AMANDA HARRIS

SLIP

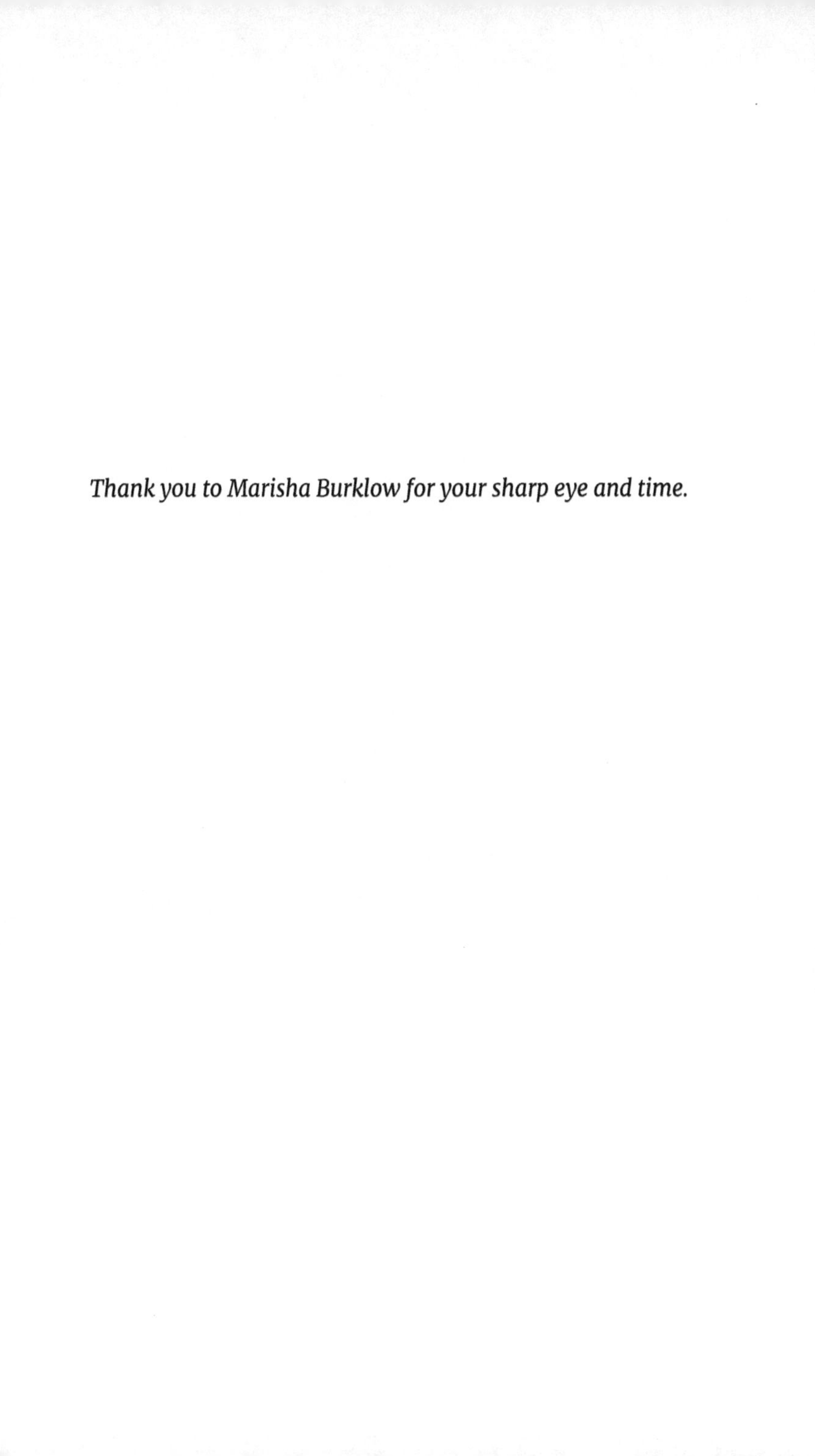

Thank you to Marisha Burklow for your sharp eye and time.

Preface

How do I tell my story when it is not mine alone to tell? How do I tell the truth when it is only the truth as I see it? I don't know how to tell the truth about all the people I fall into. I don't even know how to tell the truth about the lives of my parents even though we have been together nearly every day for the past seventeen years. All I can do is tell my own story, the way I see things. I wonder if I lie even to myself.

I don't have an it all started when moment. I could say that it started the first time I slipped out of my own body into a stranger, but that has been happening for as long as I remember. It would be like asking me about my first steps or the first time I drank from a cup. Perhaps my story starts the day my sister Maggie died, but that feels like more of an ending than a beginning. If I were less pragmatic I would say it started the day Robert took me out behind the gym, but I can't see my life story beginning with a boy. I would like to hope there is more to me than that. I think no one's life story starts at one pivot point alone. We all fall into our stories a drop at a time until the bucket is full. Most end the same way, one little drop of life at a time. Rarely do things come to a screaming halt, nor do they begin that way. So I guess I will do my best to tell the story of how I came to tear apart my life and rebuild it from the ashes.

It is my life, but it is not mine alone. This is the story of everyone I slip into, everyone I interact with daily. If I have learned anything at all it is that we are not alone. What we do, everything we do, matters. One pivot point would be the day I first slipped into Kara.

Chapter 1

I only know one thing. I need to run. Keep running. Run even more. The body I'm in already has adrenaline coursing through it. I can feel her terror. I know better than to stop but I try to evaluate my situation. I know only that I have to keep going. I dare to glance behind me and see a figure lurch forward. He misses me so I keep pushing my feet against the ground and tearing through the weeds and briers that slice at my skin. When I know that I can't run another step I duck for cover under a Magnolia tree surrounded by saplings. I tuck myself up against the trunk behind the smaller shoots and try not to breathe too noisily. All I can think about is how it would be a good time to return to my own body.

Right now!

It doesn't matter how much I want to leave, I can't control when I return to myself any more than I could control how I ended up here. I try not to scream as saplings spread apart but I let out a little yelp anyways. I toy with the bracelet on my host's wrist that has the name Kara etched into the silver. The man is saying something to me, trying to coax me closer, but his words don't match his eyes. I stand up to realize that I must be in a child's body because the man looms much taller than me.

"Come on sweetie, I'll take you home to your mama." The

man moves in and my fear turns to anger. How dare this creep corner a small girl in the woods? I don't have forever to save her, so I think fast.

"Listen to me," I command trying my best to sound formidable, "I know who you are and I have told everyone all about you. They will know everything if you don't turn around." It was a lie but I had to scare the man away from the little girl.

My words seem to spur him on though. A light dawns in his eyes. He peers into my face for a moment and I try to show him that he would find no fear in my eyes. Then, just as he was about to say something else I am gone from him and back in my own body riding shotgun in my Mom's SUV on the way to cheer practice.

"Mom," I choke out without meaning to.

"Miranda, what is it?" she asked without taking her eyes off the road.

I tell her I didn't know what was wrong. What am I supposed to say? That I need to slip back into a little girl to save her from a kidnapper in the middle of the woods? That I'm full of fear and rage because I'm worried about her and there is nothing I can do about it? No, I could not say any of that because my parents and I don't talk about my slipping away into other people. We don't talk about anything deeper than how dinner tasted and where I need to be driven through the week. I try to push the little girl in the woods from my mind because there was nothing I could do about it anyways.

"Well, you've been a silly goose all evening."

"I don't know what you mean." I stare out the window and wonder if she finally noticed that I was not really there.

"For one thing it is nice to see you off your silly diet, you polished off a whole box of Oreo Cookies. I thought milk made you nauseous before practice, but it is nice to see you drinking something wholesome. I'm certainly not complaining, we haven't had a chat like that over cookies since you were a little girl."

I choose not to reply. Mom enjoyed an evening spent with some kid more than she did when I was there, and she didn't even notice my absence as usual. At least Kara got to spend her time eating cookies and feeling safe. I hope that she ended up getting away from the man or at least slipped away again if he got her. Cheer practice was uneventful and I didn't leave myself again. I fell asleep that night wondering if the little girl was all right and if she had someone to talk to about slipping.

I never spoke to anyone about it except my sister Maggie. My parents never brought it up and by the time I realized that everyone didn't do it, it was already as natural to me as breathing.

Sometimes I did it in my sleep. I just slipped away into another life. It's not as scary as it sounds. I would go into someone else who was also sleeping, and then return to my own body and bed without even thinking about the difference. I would know, you always know right away when you are in a different body, but it doesn't hurt. It is natural. Slipping is not scary or weird at all. Each night I tell myself this. One day I will believe it.

Chapter 2

Kara tried to be brave. After all, what she did made her different, made her special. She tried not to think of all the things that man could do to her. She spent too much of her life as someone else. She never had to experience the things she heard spoken of but she still knew far more than she should.

Those things ran through her mind and kept her heart pounding hard in her chest. If only she walked straight home after school. If only she ran the other way when the hair on her arm stood on end instead of trying to figure out why she suddenly felt so afraid.

Kara started to peel the decals off her TwinkleToe Sketchers, popping each shiny bauble off without realizing she was doing it. She remembered making her mom buy them for her last week, or was it last month? She could not be sure anymore. Now she destroyed them in a nervous fit. This is what made her finally break down. The tears streamed down her face making clean lines in the layer of grime she accumulated since her captivity.

Then she started laughing. It was funny that her shoes would bring her to tears when she had not cried since her abduction two days ago. Or was it three? She knew herself well enough to know she wasn't crying over the shoes, and her tired mind found the situation hilarious.

Then she heard footsteps. She knew it would be him again and she swallowed her giggles and sobs. This time the fear didn't take hold as tight. She huddled into the corner and squeezed her eyes shut as she listened to him manipulate the lock on the door

Chapter 3

Kara stayed on my mind non-stop after that first slip into her life. All week I felt her fear. How could I not? What could I do about it when I've left myself hundreds of times? Sometimes the events I fall into are memorable, often they are boring. This is the only time it has been terrifying. Each night I wake up with a start covered in sweat because of nightmares about the man's face peering down at me. All I can do is worry and wonder. Is she okay? Did she get away? I was so lost in thought about Kara that I didn't hear whatever it was Mr. Johnston asked me.

I give him a blank look, then I flip my hair off my shoulder, "So sorry, could you repeat the question?" I grin when I hear Andrew snicker. It's not uncommon for me to suddenly show back up into my life and not know what is going on, so I have got the ditsy blond shtick down to a science. No one questions me too deeply anyways. I guess they just wrote me off as the airhead. I don't really care, as long as they don't know the truth.

When the class is over I pull out my planner. Even though the school year was mostly over I always keep my planner with a detailed schedule and map of the school available. If anyone asks about it I simply brush it off as being bad with directions and always late. The truth is, I didn't want whoever slips into my life to screw it up. As I said, I can't even remember the first time I left my body and by the time I realized everyone didn't do it, it was already the norm for me. If it were not for my sister Maggie, I would have gone crazy trying to figure out why I was so different.

Maggie and I were Irish Twins, born exactly one year apart. She knew everything about me and always balanced me when I started to feel like it was all out of control.

Now Maggie was gone and some little girl named Kara haunted my mind. I wish I knew how she ended up, but there was no control over the slip. I likely would never be her again. I just had to forget the fear I felt that day. The past few years taught me that it is best to push intrusive thoughts out of my mind. Don't dwell. Move on. Easier said than done but at least I had some practice.

Chapter 4

Robert Matthews left his own body during third period. He found himself in someone else driving down the interstate in a huge semi. The song *Midnight Rider* blared on the radio and Robert knew that his host was right in the middle of enjoying his job. He almost felt bad about sticking the poor guy in his place, but not really. Senior year in a small town high school was so dry.

Every day he put in his hours, earned his grades, and returned home. He'd been in enough bodies to know it was never going to change. He spent the last twelve years of his life working for a grade and figured he would spend the next forty working for a paycheck. He turned the radio up and started to sing along. He didn't return to his own life for several hours.

Chapter 5

I navigate the crowded halls between my two best friends. Shannon, Jules, and I became close at cheer camp the summer after Maggie died. I know if I was not on the squad they would not talk to me at all, but it's nice to call them mine just the same. Shannon is complaining about her grade in her AP science and then suddenly I'm sitting in a quiet room at a huge table surrounded by men in business suits.

I pick up the stationary laid out in front of me, the words *Benton and Bradley Law Firm* are set in gold letters across the top. My host is likely a lawyer, but what's her name? I bend down to the black leather bag leaning on my chair and peek inside for a planner. I found a laptop and a cell phone. I know it would not be okay to open one of those up in the meeting so I scooted my chair out, ready to excuse myself. Then I notice a tattoo written in dark ink across my host's wrist, the word June with a small diamond shape next to it. I took a few slow breaths to calm down a bit and hoped that no one would call upon her for anything. I pick up the pen and try to take notes for when June and I trade back. I glance up and notice a man old enough to be my dad grinning at me. I glare at him. Yuck.

Then remember that I'm June. For all I knew this guy was her crush. Why could it not have been the young lawyer next to the old geezer grinning at me suggestively? I smile at him and hope that June is taking good notes in my science class. The way I see it, the golden rule is never more applicable than in my unique situation. After all, whoever I'm in is in my body as well, and I never know if I will pass through the same host again. It does not happen regularly but often enough that revenge could be exacted if someone royally screwed up someone's life during the time they were visiting.

I stand to leave before the leering man had a chance to pursue after the meeting. To my horror, the creep reached for June's bag right before I could get it, "Let me carry that for you hon."

Before I could reply I was back in my class in front of three pages of neat handwriting.

"Wow, Miranda you're on a roll today." Shannon eyed the detailed notes that June wrote while she was in my place.

"Yeah, my dad said I would have to give up cheer practice if I didn't bring up my grades," the lie seemed to appease her. The truth was my grades never dipped below 3.6 and I held at 4.0 more often than not.

"Oh, that would so suck. I would totally quit cheering without you," Shannon vowed just as the bell rang. I put away the notes and folded my planner open on the page with my bus number on it.

The fact that I'm still riding the bus as a senior was something that my Dad and I argue about constantly. As a child psychologist, he seems to think whatever hair-brained idea he comes up with was the law. He has the idea that if I get a car before I graduate I would be spoiled beyond repair. So I get to ride the bus every day, just to go home long enough to do my homework and have Mom drive me all the way back to school for cheer practice. Even though we live ten miles away from school. None of this makes any sense to me but there is no arguing with Dad when he makes up his mind. When I argue that I need a car to get to practice, he simply suggests that I quit if it is that difficult to ride back into town.

That is not an option. Sometimes I think cheering is the only thing that keeps me sane. At first, it was just something I did to fit in, I thought it would make me more like a normal girl. I quickly found out that cheering is not just yelling helpful things, it is a sport, and the hours I spend practicing the moves keep my mind off of all the things in life I can't control. It is the one thing that is all mine.

Maggie would have teased me for it but she's not here to scoff and I need the distraction. District competitions and football games keep me busy on weekends, and camp keeps me busy in the summer. As long as I stay busy I don't think of Maggie, or slipping, or anything at all if I can help it. Cheering and slipping sometimes clash but I only left myself during game time twice. The first time whoever traded with me just ran off-field. They all teased me afterward about really having to pee, but I was grateful that the person didn't try to cheer when they couldn't. The other time I guess my guest knew the moves because no one seemed to notice.

Sometimes that makes me angrier than anything else. Even if I don't want anyone to know I'm different, it still stings that no one notices when I'm not there. When I got home I pulled my journal out from under my mattress. I have kept a record of most slips that I have had for the past seven years. This was Maggie's idea, to get them all down, because we both agreed that I could not tell our parents. I read through Dad's textbooks that he keeps in his office and I knew what happened to people with crazy claims they could not prove. I would be locked away at the worst or snickered about at least. No, thank you.

Mom and Dad are not the worst parents. On the surface, they seem great. Mom is a kindergarten teacher, and Dad is a child psychologist. Really, how lucky can I be? Before Maggie died we were a normal family. Without Maggie, it is as though they are robots just going about their daily lives doing what they always did without any heart. It is hard to explain, but it's like we are all strangers sharing life without knowing each other at all. They fit the mold of the perfect small-town family, but it feels like a lie when we sit down to dinner and can barely make small talk. It feels like a lie when they never notice the fact that sometimes I was not there at all.

I didn't slip again that day. The next morning while on the bus ride to school, I slipped into someone who was sleeping in. There are some upsides to this life.

* * *

Immediately after returning from my morning host, I went again. This is highly unusual. It took me a moment to get orientated. The first thing I noticed was sparkly shoes illuminated by a stream of dim light coming in from under a door. It's dark in the rest of the little room and my host is huddled against the wall holding her legs to her chest. Then it is over.

Just like that, I'm back in class. I look around to try to catch up with what I have missed. I feel like everyone is staring at me. It is not everyone though, just Robert Matthews. I roll my eyes at him and try to figure out what page we are supposed to be on.

12

There is nothing obviously wrong with Robert, but he has a chip on his shoulders so big I don't know how he walked upright. I know I can come off like a total bitch but I couldn't stand the idea of whoever I had slipped into giving him the wrong idea. I work hard to blend in, and he was just as out as you could get. It is not that he was not handsome. Even Shannon admitted one night during truth or dare that she thought he was hot. But he had such a wall up around himself, I doubt he even realized any of us attended school with him at all. He moved to our town in ninth grade and I don't think he had a single friend. That seemed to be the way he wanted it. Until now. Why was he staring at me?

The bell rang and I was in such a hurry to leave before he could get to me that I forgot to pull out my planner. Then I slipped again, back into the little room. This was getting weird. I can feel her fear instantly. I try to ignore the sharp stab of pain I feel in her gut. Was this hunger? Was she being starved? I try the door, but it does not budge and panic starts to swell. I feel along the walls in the tiny room and realize that I must be in a closet. The panic finally engulfs me and I try to scream but discover that my voice is spent, I can barely get a hoarse yelp out. I hear footsteps coming down a hallway and the door handle rotates. I huddle down into a corner and try to make myself smaller.

I open my eyes and I'm behind my school gym where some kids go to hang out between classes.

"Miranda?" Robert is studying me like a bug. How did I end up back here? I don't have time to worry about that, I need to get back into Kara before that door opens. I can't stand the idea of the little girl getting hurt because I was too noisy in her body. I squeeze my eyes shut again, but when I open them I'm still me.

"What's going on with you?"

"I don't know what you're talking about," I step away from him and reach into my bag for my planner.

"Okay," there was acid in his reply.

"Okay," I reply with equal venom and stalk off. I can't help but feel that there is something in the way he looked at me, something in the way he said okay that said he knew more than he let on but would play dumb if I needed him to. Could he know about what I am? No. No way, I decide.

I breeze into the second period fifteen minutes late with an airy excuse. Most teachers typically let me be once they see that my grades are better than my behavior. I plop down in the back of the class and try not to think of the little girl in the closet.

Of course, I could not get Kara out of my head. Who could? I have slipped into other people all my life so I guess I adapted to pushing worries and fears aside as I went about putting on the show of being normal. Slipping in and out of so many situations you learn quickly that there is not much you can do, and slowly you become a spectator. I figured out fast that I was not there to fix whatever issues they are having in their lives, just visiting and moving on. This time it was different. This time it was a little girl. A girl who may end up dead or who knows what else he was doing to her. I shook off the thought and debated calling the cops. How would that call go? I wondered. If I knew the location of the girl, or her last name, or her captor's name-anything at all to tell them aside from there is a girl being held captive somewhere by someone, then I would call. I don't think anyone would believe me, yet I could not stand doing nothing at all.

I never met another person who slips face to face. I mean obviously, they existed, we were trading after all, but I never had anyone to talk to who went through it. Maggie knew about it but didn't actually do it. I wished I could ask my parents for advice on what to do about missing her. I felt so helpless. I guess I started getting lost inside myself as the days went by.

Shannon noticed my mood. I didn't really care if my friends thought I was being rude though. Who cares about a reputation when a little girl was starving in a dark closet? Each day that I didn't do something I sank deeper and deeper.

"Is this about Maggie?" Shannon asked me quietly over lunch. I was surprised she remembered my sister. Shannon and I were not exactly friends when Maggie was alive, it was not until after the accident that I tried out for the squad. When she leaned in to hug me I broke into tears, I was so ashamed but I guess it was all building up. I clasped my fingers tight against my palms in an attempt to focus the panic I felt away. When I realized I was about to start sobbing out loud I stood up and rushed from the lunchroom. I guess I would let her think it was about Maggie. What was one more lie after all? I made my way down the breezeway and into the woods behind my school hoping no one would notice me.

No one did. I fell to my knees once I got into the tree line, gasping for breath. I felt like I would never stop crying, never be able to catch my breath. Then I would feel overwhelming guilt because I had no right to be the one to lose it, not when I was the one with freedom. Suddenly I was working behind the counter at a fast-food restaurant. I still felt like I was crying, but the body I was in was holding it together. I took a man's twenty and handed him back the change that was printed on the screen. By the time I finished the shift, my problems were pushed to the back of my mind by the monotonous work.

When I slipped back into my own body that evening I was home again working on my math homework at my desk. I looked down at the half-completed paper and felt grateful to have traded my life half the day. I stepped out of my room for dinner. If my parents noticed anything off about me they didn't say. It was for the best anyways, I guess. I ate when I was in my host's body, and although physically it didn't fulfill this body I still didn't have an appetite.

"I don't know what I think about you hanging out with that boy, Miranda," Mom seemed hesitant, not that I had a clue what she was hedging at anyway.

"What boy?"

"The one you were talking to after practice. What was wrong with Mark? He seemed a lot better for you," she searched my face.

What was I supposed to say when I didn't even know who she was talking about? Where did she get the idea that Mark was good for anyone? We sort of dated in eighth grade, but now he was on the verge of dropping out and losing his football scholarship because he got a freshman pregnant and his parents made him get a job.

"Don't worry about it. I'm sure it was just a one-time thing. He just needed advice about our history class." My answer seemed to appease her but still didn't tell me who the heck she was talking about. I excused myself to my room. I knew I didn't have to worry about her coming into the room I used to share with Maggie. Neither of my parents set foot in my room since the accident.

The next day when Mom dropped me off at practice Robert was waiting at the field. After she pulled away I followed him behind the bleachers before my coach noticed that I arrived.

"What do you want with me?" I demanded as soon as we were alone.

"She told me."

"Who told you what?" I spat the words at him. He was breaking into the biggest secret I ever had. I dreamed of the moment when I could tell someone the truth but I didn't picture the person I finally let in being him.

"Stop playing games. Neither of us wants to do this but if we are going to help her we need to be honest. Unless you would rather leave her there than be seen talking to me?"

"Tell me what you think you know."

He eyed me for a moment then sank down in the grass across from me, "I always thought you were one of us but it is not one of those things you ask. I mean what if you really were just the biggest ditz on the planet?"

I rolled my eyes.

"The other day in homeroom you kept grinning at me like you had some secret joke. That is when I knew you were a slider, that is the only explanation for you to blatantly flirt with me in front of your friends."

I didn't know what to say and was ashamed to admit that I was embarrassed at the thought of flirting with him without knowing it. My friends probably thought I was teasing though.

"So I went to approach you to find out if you were hosting someone I knew. When you turned away I knew you were back and went to back off, then you slipped again. I will never forget the look that little girl put on your face."

"Okay, say I believe you. What can we do?" I still could not let him know he was right.

"There is nothing to believe, we both know what you are.

What I am. You can trust me with your secret Miranda because it is mine too."

"So how do I get back to Kara?" I nervously tore at a blade of grass and tried to pretend that talking about this out loud was not the most embarrassing, exhilarating thing that ever happened. It was as if someone released a pressure valve on me that I didn't know existed. I felt light and dizzy.

"I have not perfected it but I think I can teach you."

"Did she tell you anything that could lead us to her?"

"She had you shaking like a leaf so I led you/her to the back of the gym. When we got there I told her to calm down and tell me her name. She told me Kara Roth and she said she was scared he was going to hurt her. That is all I got before you came back. Then yesterday I searched for you but you were someone else. I did hang out with you for a bit though."

"Robert! That's huge! We can find her now." I stood up, excited to finally have something tangible to work with.

"No, it is not that simple. Yes, now we know who she is, but does that answer where she is? Who has her? How to get her back?" Robert started pacing with me and rambled on about his efforts, "I searched for her name and she is officially a missing person. Her parents are beside themselves and the police have no leads."

"We need to call them!" I pulled out my phone.

Robert snatched it away, "and say what? I don't have to tell you how crazy we'll come across, and if we do know anything that we can't explain, they will think we did it."

I yanked my phone back. "Okay, so what do we do?"

"You need to get back to her and get her out of there, or at least find out who has her."

"No kidding, well let me tap my ruby slippers together until

I am her again!”

"I don't think that will work," Robert deadpanned.

"I have to go, my Mom will be here any minute and I need to be with the squad before she gets here."

"Yeah, we would not want you to miss a practice. I mean what is one more dead little girl compared to team spirit?"

"You bastard, you have no clue who I am so don't–" I quit talking when I realized that he was gone and someone else was staring back at me through his eyes. The person just stared politely, waiting for me to finish my tirade. I'm not sure exactly how I knew Robert was gone, but I had no doubt that he was replaced. It was eerie to be on the other side for once.

Later that night the words "one more dead girl" kept me awake. What did he mean one more?

Chapter 6

When Robert returned he found himself wandering around the school grounds in the dark. The crickets and the sprinkler system were deafening after the silence of his host's life. He quickly got in his truck and headed towards home. He didn't see himself as rebellious, although it drove his parents crazy that he would not keep his name and other information in plain sight. He found it amusing to know that whoever slipped into him would be lost for the time.

He could not bring himself to care about what people thought about his behavior when he was not even in his own body. The risk factor of not knowing exactly what he would return to gave him a thrill. He also didn't like the idea of just anyone he hosted knowing everything about his life, somehow not letting them know who they were and what they should do when they 'visited' made him feel in control. His dad understood because he tried to soothe his mom when she would give him a lecture about it. When he got home his dinner was cold in the microwave but his mother sat in the dim kitchen at the table, still up waiting for him.

"Robert?" she asked.

"It's me, ma. I told you that you don't need to wait up." He hugged her and noticed in the journal that she always kept on her. She wrote her list in bullet points:

- Waiting up for my son Robert.
- Don't nag at him, welcome him home.
- His dinner is in the microwave.

Robert smirked at her. She made it a point to always be so careful with her notes that she never let anyone that she hosted shirk during their time in her life. If she were doing housework she would list her chores down to the minute detail in front of her. When she slipped away there was no excuse not to continue doing whatever she was doing at the time.

"You know I did," Jillian said then she kissed his cheek.

"How was your day?"

"Not awful. How's Rachael?" Robert eyed his sister's doorway.

"She had a good day, she slipped into a beauty pageant and her host won first place. The girl was shining all day after that. She is likely still up, you should go to her."

He walked to his sister's room and found her asleep. She was still grasping her book of short stories by O. Henry, Robert didn't know how she got into them but she said she found them addictive and would always try to get him to read them for the twist endings and the random details of the era. For that, Robert was grateful and would have given O. Henry the world if he could because those stories entertained his sister for hours.

Seeing Rachael in pain tore Robert to pieces. Sometimes he felt like he took her chemo harder than she did. She acted so strong even when her body was weak. He wanted to reach down and stroke her face but he would not wake her for anything so he tip-toed out of her room turning off the light behind him.

With all the problems that slipping caused in his life, Robert still would not change it about his family. If it got Rachael out of her pain-filled body for even a moment, he would embrace it wholeheartedly. Not that he had a choice, slipping was like walking for him as well, he could not even remember the first time he did it and didn't put too much thought into it when it happened.

Chapter 7

I searched for Robert the next day, but he was absent. I spent my time trying to slip into Kara by keeping her on my mind. I didn't have any success though, in fact, I didn't slip into anyone at all that day. Some days were like that. Sometimes I didn't go for days at a time, for so long that I would begin to question my sanity and wonder if it all was just some childhood fantasy that I made up. I would begin to have hope for a normal life then I would slip into someone and realize that I was not insane or delusional, but still a freak.

The day seemed to go on and on. If there was one positive thing about my non-static lifestyle it would be that it cured boredom. When I got home I told my Mom I had a headache and could not go to practice. I knew that skipping practice twice in a week could get me suspended, and I felt a little guilty for lying, but I had to do something towards finding Kara.

I spent the evening searching online for Kara Roth. My heart shattered for her family. The pictures of her standing with her backpack on the first day of fourth grade gave me chills. Her dark eyes seemed to bore right through me. There had to be something I could do to save her.

Suddenly I was in a bedroom. There was a Harry Styles poster on the wall and a vanity piled high with makeup and hats. I slipped into some girl's room. I decided to lay down and take a nap in the small pink bed until I was back home, I felt extremely tired. I stood to turn out the light and noticed Robert sitting in a chair tucked into the corner.

"Did it work?" he looked at me expectantly.

"Did what work? Why are you here?"

"This is my sister's room. Now let's get to work."

As the meaning of his words sunk in, my own started spilling out, "you mean she has it too? Do your parents trade with others as well? How long have you known? Wow! I wonder if my parents have it? Why don't my parents talk about it?" I knew I was babbling but I could not seem to keep the words in. I never met someone who did what I did, and now I find out that there are two in one family in my hometown. I was buzzing with the implications.

"I doubt your parents know if they have not talked to you about it Miranda and if they don't know you need to prepare yourself for the fact that one or both of them are not your blood relatives because this is hereditary." Robert studied me as his words sunk in. I felt the blood drain from my borrowed face. The room seemed to spin. But he kept staring and I knew I needed to keep it together. I could fall apart over this in my own time.

"So why am I here and what did you mean when you asked me if it worked?" I tried to flip his sister's hair but discovered that there was none there. I moved to the vanity mirror and inspected the peach fuzz growing in on top of her head over swollen pink scar tissue.

"Oh. Robert, I'm sorry. What kind?" I met his eyes in the mirror.

"It's called a Glioblastoma Multiforme Tumor or GBM for

short, and she will be fine. It is in remission. She does not need your charity or pity," Robert snapped.

I didn't reply.

"I need you to listen before you leave. You can get into Kara at will if you will do what I say."

I stared at him and tried to focus, he just dropped two bombs into my life and either didn't know or didn't care that I was reeling from the blast.

"The first thing I need you to do is focus. Focus on your feelings right before you leave your body. It's not obvious, and you won't always notice even when you are more in tune because most people don't often have states of emotional flux. But when they do, and when you slip at the same time you can sense them before you go. If you try really hard. So that is what I want you to do."

"That's it? Concentrate on my emotions, make sure they are my own?"

"That's it for now. The point is training your brain to recognize a slip as something to notice. We have been doing this for so long that it is like asking your body to notice digestion or breathing. It is possible, but you have spent years ignoring all symptoms of it. You're not going to suddenly be able to do it overnight."

"How do you know I will be able to do it at all? Why don't you do it?"

"When Rachael was getting her brain scans she had a slip. It showed up on the MRI. My Dad was friends with the oncologist and he sneaked her in after-hours for a few practice runs, she eventually learned to recognize when her spirit was leaving through visual representation. She has been trying to teach me but it is not the same. Even if I could learn to slip at will I can't slip into Kara either way." Robert spoke of it all so matter of fact.

I desperately wanted to actually meet his sister, not just borrow her body. And his parents too. I could not fathom a whole family of people who left their bodies just like I did. I felt a pang of jealousy towards them, then I was back in my room sitting at my vanity. I had to laugh when I saw that Robert's sister had set my hair in curlers and slathered some of my mom's night cream on my face. I debated confronting my parents about what Robert said but suddenly felt too weary to get into all of it.

I didn't want to hurt them either. After Maggie, they didn't deserve any more drama. I fell asleep trying not to think about them, or the possibility that I was adopted. I know it was a lot to push aside but I had a whole lifetime of practice.

Chapter 8

"Thank you, Rachael. I will not ask you to do that again," Robert leaned down and kissed his sister on the cheek then turned to go.

"I don't mind, her hair is fun to play with and she has the best books. Maybe you can ask her to borrow some for me?"

"Yeah, sure." Robert turned to go wondering what his genius sister and the head of the cheer squad could read in common.

"Robert?" Rachael called before he could shut the door, "she is not as bad as you think."

"Excuse me?"

"I know you think she is just some shallow girl without a soul, but remember when you went through your goth stage before we moved here? That is all her cheer outfit and carefree attitude is for her, a mask. Cut her some slack. Alright?" Rachael snuggled down into her purple comforter and mumbled goodnight.

He stood there in the doorway wondering how his kid sister managed to be so intuitive about people. She typically nailed a person's personality down instantly, it was one of her many gifts. Her parents trusted her judgment without question. Sometimes Robert wondered if she was not hosting some ancient spirit or maybe Yoda from Star Wars. The girl was too wise for her frail body and fifteen years but in this case, she was way off base. He could not get her words out of his mind. She always saw right through Robert with a glance. What if she was right about Miranda?

Robert rolled his eyes and pretended to be annoyed. He could not suppress his grin though. Today his family went to Rachael's doctor together to get the results of her latest blood work. It seemed that the surgery to remove her tumor went exactly as planned and she just had a few more chemotherapy appointments. They were warned not to put too much stock in preliminary reports. Hope-yes, reliance-no, but Robert felt like a lead weight had been lifted from his gut. He could not lose his little sister, and after today he had reason to believe that he would not. He didn't let the word relapse even enter his vocabulary.

* * *

I made the effort to notice pre-slip signs but I was in the host body before I knew it each time. It was never Kara. Robert didn't speak to me in school and since I didn't have any news about Kara or my progress I didn't feel the need to approach him.

I tried to put what he said about slipping being hereditary and the implications for my parents if that were true out of my head, but I kept thinking about it although I was never brave enough to mention it to them.

I slipped during dinner that evening and returned after the dishes were done. I was so disappointed because they were having lasagna, my favorite, but my body felt full so I could not justify another plate. One of the downsides of slipping was that you could not technically control what someone did when you hosted them. It was not a problem generally, but sometimes the little things piled up. I would not write on my hand I love lasagna please don't fill up my body with so many calories that I cannot taste any myself, but I wanted to. I couldn't really get mad at the guest for acting normal yet for some reason I felt like crying. It was stupid and silly. I knew this but still, I wanted to throw a temper tantrum.

Then I was being tucked in by a stranger. I looked around at the room and decided that my host must be six or seven. The child was angry and in the middle of kicking off her covers when I took over.

"Claire, I need you to go to bed now. Grandma's coming tomorrow we have to get up early to pick her up from the airport," the woman looked desperate and I vowed never to have children if this was what it was all about.

"Alright, Mama. Goodnight," I snuggled down into the covers and tried to get the body I was in to sleep before the brat returned. I felt a hand turn me over.

"Is she gone?" the mother whispered peering into my eyes.

"Um, yes," I said sitting up.

"Oh, thank God. I try to be patient but she was trying me tonight. Who are you?"

"I'm Miranda, um I'm seventeen. She will be safe at my house my parents are great."

"They are in for a treat. I hope she doesn't give them too much trouble. Tell them thank you and I'm sorry for me when you get back will ya?"

I felt I was dreaming, how could this woman be so open about slipping? How did she know? I went from thinking that it was something each person kept to themselves to having two people address me in two days. It felt surreal.

"They don't know I'm not me right now. Whatever she does they will think I did. How bad is she?"

"How would your parents not know you're gone?"

"They never know, I thought everyone kept it secret." I felt vulnerable and hated that I was about to cry in front of this lady who just got pardoned from dealing with a crying child. I blinked back her tears, "Well let's get this body to sleep before she returns to it."

"Oh honey, you're adopted. I should have known. My name is Mary Anders I live in Seattle, Washington. Do you think you can remember that? Look me up online, I would love to chat."

I could not reply, I only lay there silently crying with my back turned toward her.

"Goodnight Sweetie," Mary quietly crept out of the room.

I woke up the next morning in my bed. On the walls in my favorite shade of M.A.C. lipstick was a crude drawing of a family with two kids and a dog. I rolled my eyes and went to the shower. My room was going to have to wait. I had to find Robert.

Chapter 9

Conner Adams didn't want to accept the hand the fates dealt him, but the cards didn't surprise him. What did surprise him was the nine happy years he did have. Nine years were not enough though. So many times during those nine years he waited for the other shoe to drop. He didn't feel worthy of Nina's love, but when she said she would marry him he knew he was the happiest man on earth.

He often felt small to the task of being a father to his two beautiful daughters, but he adored them all to the point of worship. Towards the end, his life with his girls was so perfect he knew it had to be a dream. Then the dream ended, and he became stuck in a nightmare world, a world that appeared to be the same as before but everything was a struggle. The job he loved, as a small-town sheriff's deputy, suddenly became unbearable. His favorite food tasted like garbage. Everything in life was broken on the day his wife and daughters died in a head-on collision with a drunk driver.

Conner never had a sense that he deserved his family. Early on his father made it clear to him that he was unworthy of anything other than maybe a kick in the ribs when he was already down. Then he married Nina, and while he did not believe that he deserved his girls, but he knew that he could never live without them. All his years as a boy his father never broke him. He was either ignored completely or used as a punching bag, depending on how much the old man had to drink. His mother ran off at some point when he was a toddler. The old man loved to tell him how much she could not stand to change his crappy diapers and that Conner was the singular reason she was gone. Since Conner could not come up with a memory of her to prove otherwise he figured the old man must be telling the truth, that there was something unlovable, something unworthy in him. Something so bad that even his mother had to get away as soon as she could.

When his dad died during Conner's senior year, he didn't feel relieved, but he could not bring himself to cry either. He simply joined the Marine Corps and went to war, putting his crappy childhood behind him. It was right after 9/11 and joining felt like the right thing to do.

After serving his four years in the military he found Nina. She just graduated from college and was teaching second grade. They met when he pulled her over for speeding to work one morning. It was ten o'clock and she had to be going eighty. When he handed her the ticket she seemed to be truly repentant.

"I seemed to be out of myself this morning officer, and when I came back I was three hours late for work. I teach second grade and well, there was no phone and I could not call." She looked so earnest that he could not bring himself to mention that he noticed the cell phone on the seat next to her. He didn't give her a ticket that day, and a week later when he was assigned to safety day at her school she asked him on a date.

After that they were inseparable. When she became pregnant he begged her to marry him. The only flaw he could find in Nina was that sometimes she was distant. He could not place his finger on it but there were times when she seemed to be playing a role, and then as suddenly as the feeling came on it was gone and he would wonder what he thought he saw, to begin with. Then one day after Gracie was born, Nina told him that sometimes she slipped away, that sometimes she traded bodies with other women. She confessed that she thought their baby must do it too, but she could not tell for sure. Conner called the psychologist. He figured she must be having some sort of postpartum depression linked mental breakdown. After a few visits, Nina never mentioned trading with other people again.

Eventually, he forgot she ever said it at all. Then eight years later those words in that moment early in their marriage broke apart the crack that formed in him when he lost his whole family. Those words, that idea that she and their daughters may not have been in their bodies when they died became the only thing that got him out of bed each morning. It kept him going and drove him crazy at the same time.

Chapter 10

Robert was closed off in homeroom. I was unsure if he was in there or someone else so I let him be for the moment. After class he seemed to know where he was going so I pursued him.

"I think I felt it," I said but he kept walking.

"I felt like throwing myself on the ground and screaming, then I was a tantrum-throwing six-year old named Clair. I never realized my feelings were not my own all the time. It is bad enough to trade all the time, now I find out my emotions are not mine either-" When I heard my voice crack I stopped talking. Robert stopped walking and studied me like I was a toad.

"Come with me," he said curtly. I followed him out the door. When we reached the back of the gym Robert looked around the corner to make sure no one was listening.

"Okay, now that you recognize pre-slip you need to control it a little. It's not possible to have complete control but you can have a little say in what happens. One time I actually stopped a slip altogether but I have not been able to again, I think maybe it has something to do with the other slider as well. The next time you have even the slightest inkling you're going to slip try to make yourself notice every little detail. You have to get your brain to react when it happens so you start having physical signs."

"Okay, how is that going to help me?"

"My dad has been researching the possibility of controlling a slip and he came across a study that showed people on an MRI where their brain perceives pain. When people were able to see their brain and the pain on a screen they were able to control the pain."

"Well I don't have an MRI in my closet, do you?" I snapped.

"No, Miranda, I don't. Just bear with me for a minute before you put back on the super bitch mask okay?"

His words stung but I didn't retort.

"Okay, so the idea is to train your brain to give you better signs of a slip. We have been slipping for as long as we remember so it comes naturally, you have to make it unnatural."

"How do we do that without being able to see the part of the brain that causes the slip?"

"First off try to see if you notice any signs at all. You did well noticing the tantrum of a six-year-old. Try to key on how you feel at each moment and maybe that will help. Also if you can fear a slip then maybe you will get anxious right before. The point is to be able to know exactly when it is happening in time to focus on Kara in the split second you have before you're gone."

"Have you ever done it?"

"No, I used the method to stop a slip one time and have not been able to again. My sister had a special circumstance due to her cancer. I told you before that she had extra MRI time. She is better than me and controlling her slips. As far as I know, no one else has any control."

"Well that gives me confidence," I murmured as I hurried

off, late again for another class

Chapter 11

"*My name is Kara Ann Roth. My parents call me Kara. I am ten. I am kidnapped. I don't know where I am or who took me,*" Kara repeated this mantra in her head over and over again.

She knew to get out of the situation she had to tell everyone around her the next time she slipped. She repeated her name. It helped her to stay grounded, it seemed that each day she lost a little of herself, a little of her memories, and became a shadow. She felt like dust, like she had been laying in this closet for as long as time.

When she repeated her name and mumbled to herself about her pet cat Pepper and her dog Salt or her mom and dad who helped her understand who she was even when she slipped into other people and was not ready to understand it. When she focused on these things she felt a little more consequential. Each time she slipped away she enjoyed the reprieve from the closet but felt a little more disconnected from who she was or is, or was... or is....

"*My name is Karen Ann Roth, my parents called me Kara, they call me Kara, I am ten years old...* "

Chapter 12

For the rest of the day, I didn't slip. Instead of being a relief, it made me upset. I needed to slip, needed to practice if there was any chance of gaining control and choosing Kara as a host. I went to sleep that night angry that for once my "disability" could not be ability. I would love to use it to save a little girl's life, then all these years of hiding and feeling like a freak might be worth it.

The next morning I woke up in my room feeling more than a little begrudged. I got ready for school but the effort to pick out a trendy outfit or to put my hair in body curlers hardly seemed worth it, so I just pulled on a pair of jeans with my class t-shirt and went downstairs. If my parents noticed the fact that for once my makeup was not applied perfectly or my hair was in a limp ponytail they didn't comment. I expected no less. If they didn't notice when another person took over my entire body why should they notice the small details? For an Educator and a Doctor, my parents were blind and dumb to the matter of their own lives.

I felt like a decoration to them. Much like Dad's PhD. D. on the wall in his office, or Mom's perfect garden where she held the Solar Springs Woman's Auxiliary parties every spring. As long as I was not obviously broken no one would attempt to fix me or check on me at all. Maybe it was better before Maggie died, maybe they noticed me then. I really could not remember much from before. I didn't ask them over breakfast if I was adopted. I just smiled and studied their features searching for myself in their faces.

Maggie had Mom's deep-set eyes and Dad's dark hair. I assumed I got my blond hair from her, and I assumed I got my brains from Dad. I teared up over my oatmeal, but they still didn't notice. I went back upstairs without a word and sat in my room trying not to think at all until I needed to leave for the bus stop.

Against Robert's advice, I decided to call the 800 number listed on the web for Kara's family. With a brick in my belly, I forced myself not to hang up.

"Hello, this is the Kara Roth hot line," a too cheerful voice answered.

"Um hey, I need to speak to Kara's Mom."

"I'm sorry I will be happy to take a message but she will not be talking to callers."

"I need to speak to her only. It is personal. I promise I will not be cruel." I had to wonder what kind of sickos called in to make the need for such protection.

"I'm sorry sweetie, leave a message and I will be sure to pass it," then I heard shuffling and muffled voices arguing.

"This is Carla Roth, do you have any information about my daughter?" The desperation in her voice cut to the core and stole my words for the moment.

"Hello, is anyone there?"

"Yes, I, well I slipped into Kara after she was kidnapped," I didn't say anything else. If they knew about slipping then that was enough and if not I unnecessarily hurt her. The silence seemed to stretch on forever.

"Hello?"

"Hello?"

"Hey, this is Jensen Roth, Kara's Dad. Tell me what you saw. How is she?"

"When I first met her she was running through the woods, I think they were local to my area because there were Palm fronds and Magnolias. Then a man was talking to her, trying to get her to come to him. The next two times she was in a small dark room, like a closet. She was afraid but seemed unharmed." I didn't think it useful to tell him about her hunger.

"When is the last time you were in contact?" the man's voice broke and he seemed to have trouble choking out the words. Robert was right about not calling them.

"It has been a few days, I'm sorry maybe I should not have called."

"No, I am glad you did. The next time you call ask for Jensen, Kara's mom is not like us. If you get any information at all call my cell."

I wrote down the number and tried to shake the hopelessness that seeped into my bones. Talking to Kara's parents and hearing the raw pain in their voices was hard to do. I knew after feeling the small sample of their grief through the phone that a person should never have to go through what they were enduring. I vowed to do whatever was needed to help them

Chapter 13

Robert's relief over his sister's diagnosis was not unfounded and Rachael was able to return to school within the month. Mainly because she wore her parents down once she knew she had a chance of graduating.

On her first day back to school everyone treated Rachael extra nice. They made the effort to smile at her and welcome her back. The unspoken words behind; "It's so nice to see you," were, "I am glad you are not dead." The smiles were too big and bright, they seemed ready to crack. Rachael told herself she was imagining it, still, she knew things were different now. Shortly after she had to quit school for her cancer treatments her best friend Casey told her about a new girl in class. Rachael was not daft; she knew that her friends replaced her long before she returned to school when the phone calls from classmates became less and less frequent. She believed though, that when she returned she would fit right back in. It seemed that it was not going to be as easy as she hoped. They had to pull a chair from another table for her to sit with her friends in the lunchroom and everyone smiled at her but no one seemed at ease. Rachael returned their too-bright smiles until she felt like her face would break. Then she realized that she didn't have to do this, she of all people had an out.

* * *

I had that weak feeling again, I didn't take long to realize I was Rachael for the fourth time this week. The faces around the lunch table seemed expectant and a bit nervous. Why didn't Robert tell me that it was her first day back? Then I wondered why I thought that he would bother to tell me anything about his sister. I shot my biggest Southern Smile at the group of girls and they didn't stand a chance.

"So what's new?" I tittered. I was good at putting on the public face, in fact, I made it my life. If Rachael needed my help in an awkward social situation, I was all too happy to comply.

Chapter 14

Unfortunately for Robert, the thing about Miranda is that up close beyond the perfect exterior and haughty act, she was human, nothing more and nothing less. She was vulnerable, more than Robert ever imagined, and smart, so smart she could easily be valedictorian. Yet she hid herself so well in an attempt to hide her slips that she also hid her positive side. She infuriated Robert and once again he found himself stuck in the spiral of hating that he gave a damn.

She cornered him after school behind the gym, "Robert I know this is not something you want to consider but the most logical step at this point is using Rachael to find her."

"No! No. Get that out of your mind, Miranda. She is just a girl and she has been through too much already. Shut up about it." he tried to storm off but she grabbed his shirt.

"You're not the only one who cares for Rachael. I have walked in her shoes more times than I care to count and let me tell you she is one tough cookie. I would die before hurting her any more than she has been but I don't know how to slip at will and she already proved that she has a knack for it."

"What do you mean that you have walked in 50 her shoes more times than you can count?"

"Her life is hard since she returned to school Rob, people

either tease her or treat her like an infant. You know Rachael, she is tough but sensitive to people's emotions. When things get bad she trades me for a while."

"She knows better than to do something like that. It's intrusive. When Dad coached her on how to slip at will, he lectured her for like a week about not doing it."

"Give her a break, I can handle a group of kids and she seems to like to hang out in my boring life. I don't mind. I just want you to know that I know her, I care about her, and if there were any other options I would take them but she is it."

Robert knew at that moment regardless of the consequences he had to do it. The fire in her eyes, as she argued with him, fueled him. He had to taste her lips to feel her against him. If she hated him so be it. This was worth the risk. He leaned in and felt a thrill as her eyes widened when she realized what he was going to do. Then he closed his eyes so his other senses would pick up her scent, her taste, the way her lips felt against his. He put his hand behind her neck and pressed his lips gently against hers, pushing her lips apart with his tongue. His stomach dropped to the ground when he realized that she was kissing him back. He opened his eyes for a moment and crushed her against him, both of them falling into the brick wall unaware of anything else around them. Then he was in an empty auditorium sitting in a circle listening to what appeared to be group therapy.

"Yesterday I was in line at the pharmacy for an hour, and when I finally made it to the beginning of the line, the pharmacy tech informed me that they were closing in fifteen minutes and I would have to pick up the prescription tomorrow. A month ago, I would have yelled every name in the book at her. I was still angry yesterday, but I didn't scream," a short bald man told the group proudly.

"So what did you do instead?" asked the therapist.

"This is bullshit!" Robert exploded and stormed out of the room slamming the door behind him. He paced back and forth in the hall and waited to return to his body. Kissing Miranda was worth the risk of being slapped by her but being pulled away from his body when she didn't reject him, was a pain he didn't expect. He walked the halls until he was back in his own body but she had left when he returned to the empty school.

Chapter 15

Robert stiffened in my arms then he stepped away. I stared at him for a moment then realized that he was not there anymore. I awkwardly waved goodbye without a word and ran down the hall. My mind raced all over the moment he kissed me. I never felt electricity like that before. His kiss set me on fire figuratively, sure, but at the moment I would argue that the feeling of his body against mine caused a literal ignition. I know without a doubt that he was himself when he kissed me.

I could not help but wonder if later he might deny it. I rushed to the bus and wondered the whole way home why he did it. I kept putting my hand on my lips, they felt raw and exposed as if the kiss set off a chemical reaction in my skin that made nerve endings explode. I tried to get my mind off of him, off of the way he tasted, but it was impossible. My body was too alive and each of my senses froze at that moment when he pushed me against the cold block walls and set me on fire. I thought about the other boys who kissed me. I have had boyfriends before. My friends all dated each other exclusively and no one outside our circle of friends from the football team and cheer squad. If I didn't date I would stand out and that was not something I could afford to do, but I never felt like that while being held during a school dance or clumsy kisses after a date. I never went past kissing, partly because I felt it would be humiliating to host someone else during sex but mostly because I never felt a kiss like that. I never even knew that a single moment could be so powerful that it could alter your perspective of a person.

Suddenly, Robert was not simply the infuriating loner from school and crime solver as of late, he was Robert-sigh! What had come over me? I fought to shake the feeling, fought to shake him from my mind. I just had to convince myself that logically, lust could be controlled and there was no way I would become a fool over anyone, and certainly not Robert Matthews.

Chapter 16

Kara kept repeating her name but the words were becoming meaningless sounds. If she didn't slip away she knew her sanity would have been gone a long time ago. As it was she slipped less and less. When she did she told the people around her that she had been kidnapped but they looked at her like she was crazy and laughed. Then she would be back in the closet, back inside herself, lost in the infinite space of her mind.

Occasionally he would come and stare into her eyes as if he was looking for someone, drop a bottle of water or a breakfast bar in front of her, then turn and leave. Those times were few and far between though and she could not remember the last time she ate or drank aside from the water and cereal bars. She used the bathroom in the farthest part of the small closet and sat huddled in the other corner.

* * *

On some days Conner reasoned that he never left himself in his 35 years, no one did. Then he thought about the times when he would catch her staring at him curiously and when he asked what was wrong she always told him it was nothing. Then she was gone. Gone. Forever over in a moment. One day, one moment, one idiot's bad choice and life snuffed out.

Conner was alive. His daughters and the only women he ever loved were dead, and he was alive. He continued to dwell on the image of Nina telling him about how she slipped out of her own body, and the thought became a seed of hope planted in a barren desert of despair. The seed sprouted and flourished each day as he contemplated the possibility of her still existing somewhere in some form. By the time a year passed the seed of an idea became a pine tree with a taproot running straight through his essence. He had no idea of what to do with the idea though. How do you find someone when she could be anyone? Just how do you ask a stranger if they are your wife or daughter? He didn't plan on his search getting quite so out of hand, he didn't plan on becoming the bad guy. Then one day he saw her in the smile of a diner across from him. A redhead met his eyes and smiled a slow smirk, identical to the one Nina shared with him when they had an inside joke.

"I'm sorry I didn't believe you," he choked out, stumbling towards her. The redhead's smile faded and she dropped a twenty on the table and rushed out, but Conner knew his Nina and he walked the streets for days searching for the redhead. He never saw her and vowed he would never let his girl slip away again. It was a year later when he saw his daughter, Sophie, in a little girl in her front yard. He was driving around aimlessly when he saw the girl playing on a swing set. She looked up and grinned an adorable toothless grin that only an eight-year-old can give. His heart skipped a beat when he saw recognition in her eyes and he scooped her up without a second thought.

He didn't mean to kill her. He just wanted to talk, but the

brat kept trying to run, if Sophie was ever in her she was gone now. Conner didn't give up though, oh no, he was going to find his girls and get them all back. He had to tell Nina he believed her, and that he saw Sophie.

Now he had a new girl. She was Grace, at least sometimes, he knew it. He could see in her eyes. He wished he could treat her better, but he could not risk her running, keeping her locked up tight and weak was the only way. *It is the only way*, he mumbled as he made his way to the closet. All he had to was wait for one of the people who passed through her to recognize him. Wait for her to call him daddy.

Chapter 17

The toxic smell woke me up. When I was in fourth grade my family went on a vacation to South Texas. At a gas station, the sign on the bathroom wall requested that the patrons throw the toilet paper in the trash and not flush it. The smell in the hot desert bathroom was unbearable. Now it was terrifying. Next, I noticed that it was too dark, darker than my bedroom with the seashell nightlight. I knew at that moment that I was Kara.

I started slamming her small frame into the door but had no success at all. Then I heard footsteps rushing down the hall. I started to cry out but realized that Kara's voice was completely gone and my throat was parched. The door locks began to click one by one. I was so scared I could not take my eyes off the small sliver of light coming through the bottom. I stood shaking, waiting.

* * *

Kara started yelling as soon as she woke up under the comforter. Then she noticed a glass of water on the nightstand and drank down every drop. She knew it would not help her when she returned to herself, but it felt so good. Then she resumed her screaming. When a woman and man rushed in she told them her name and that she was kidnapped. Then she was back in the closet, with *him* standing over her looking down like she was a bug to be squashed or studied idly on a hot summer day. The stare made her feel of no consequence and she read him right, as soon as he knew she was herself he turned and walked away without a word.

* * *

I returned to find both of my parents in my room staring at me. I tried not to show that I was surprised that they crossed into the space I shared with Maggie.

"Sorry, I guess I had a bad dream," I said wondering if they would buy it and hoping that they would not and maybe they would help me help Kara.

"It's okay sweetie," Mom patted my head.

"These things are normal for a young woman on the cusp of so much change," my father said. I smiled weakly as though his words helped me out. As soon as they left I called Robert's cell. He answered on the second ring as though he had been waiting for my call at three a.m.

"Robert," I whispered into the receiver.

"Did you slip into her?"

"Yes, It was so terrible, I don't think he is feeding her or letting her out at all. It smelled so bad. He opened the door and just stared at me. Then I was back in my bed. Apparently, she screamed her head off because she woke up my parents. I don't know what to do!" It all rushed out of me but just knowing he was up to date and I was not alone made me feel a bit better.

"Tomorrow after school. Tell your mom you're going home with a friend. I need you to meet my Dad," Robert didn't wait to hear me say okay before he hung up. It was alright though, I would not have argued.

* * *

Robert's family was not at all what I expected. They were so normal.Not that I expected them to be circus freaks or anything, but when he pulled up to the Tudor-style house with a pristine lawn I was floored. Most of my friends on the football and cheer squad lived in this area. I hate that my parents refused to move into town and kept us in the rural area of the county. Robert's home was showcase worthy and his mother was actually wearing an apron as she fixed dinner. She was tall and had dark hair like Robert. There was a no-nonsense way about her that intimidated me but I tried to hide it with a smile. I have to admit that I felt like Alice down the rabbit hole and I hope that it didn't show on my face that I was literally prepared to go to a trailer park to meet Robert's family. He dressed like he wore someone's hand-me-downs and he was so defensive as though he had something to hide, which technically he did. Being an outsider was, in my opinion, the exact opposite way one should hide slipping. As handsome as he was, and the fact that his family apparently had money, he could have ruled our high school if he wanted. After all, in a small town money and influence talked a lot louder than common sense. Instead, Robert wore old shoes and faded jeans, and he always kept to himself. I guess we all wear our own masks.

"Okay, my dad is a pediatrician. When Rachael got cancer he turned to his best friend, an oncologist from Gainesville. Well, Dr. Grant has let Dad in on every step of my sister's treatment, when she had to have a CT scan he actually let Dad do it each time. It became kind of a thing, he never asked why it meant so much to my Dad and Rachael to be alone during the cat scan he just left them and came back when it was over. Since Dad was a doctor no one saw it as too weird." I studied Robert as he talked and tried not to notice how handsome he was when he was not scowling at me.

"I'm telling you all this so you understand how Dad taught Rachael to control her slips. The reason Dad insisted on having the CT room to himself when she went through was because she slipped the very first time she was scanned. The slip was picked up by the scanner. So she and Dad basically took advantage of Dr. Grant and went to the scanner as much as possible until he told them to back off a bit. Anyways, by being able to actually see her brain before a slip Rachael taught her body how to recognize one. Now apparently she uses the skills to slip out on her life when the going gets tough and stick you in her shoes."

"Wow, this means so much. I wonder if there is a cure for slipping. And give her a break Robert, I can handle a bunch of teenage girls."

"I don't know. I hear they can be cruel," Robert smirked. I ignored the cut and tried to tame the flutters in my insides. Apparently, I was turning into an idiot.

"More than you know, so don't give her a hard time for switching with me whenever she needs to get away," I snapped at him trying to get myself back in balance. Robert just smiled.

"There is one problem with her *trading* with you any time she wants." He was studying me. Why was he staring at my lips?

"Wha-?" I didn't get to finish my sentence before he pressed his mouth against mine. Then my knees went weak. Surely that does not happen. His arms wrapped around my waist and pulled me to him as we both crashed down on his bed. I was drowning in the moment, in the smell of his skin, the feel of his lips and his hands, I could not have come up for air if I tried. I was lost.

"Ahem," someone cleared their throat in the hall and I was mortified to see Robert's dad walk by. I jumped away from him as though he were on fire, then I studied his eyes to see if he were himself.

"Now do you see why I'm not completely comfortable with Rachael and you trading as a habit? I'm not sure I can stop doing that."

"I'm not sure I want you to," I replied, then tried to wink to hide my surprise at my boldness. I probably looked like I had a bug in my eye.

"I assume you're Miranda, I'm Bill," Robert's Dad was friendly enough, but I was mortified. I wasn't used to being busted while making out. I wasn't used to making out at all.

Bill reminded me of my father before Maggie died. He clearly worked with children and viewed catching his son on top of a girl as a rite of passage. He probably read about how to handle the situation in a textbook on hormones. His casual attitude put me a little bit at ease. We followed him to his den and sat down across from him on a plush brown leather sofa. He placed a large envelope on the table. When I opened it I found black slides with images of a brain. I think. Not that I understood what the gray blobs meant.

"What you're seeing is a picture of Rachael's brain. On the next screen are pictures of her brain mid-slip, and the next is after a slip." I could see slight changes in an area of the center set of pictures.

"What does this mean?" I carefully placed the pictures back in the envelope and set them on the coffee table.

"As soon as Rachael and I realized that we could see physical evidence of a slip, we knew we had to try to find a way to notice them enough to control them." Bill was looking at me expectantly but I was unsure what to say. What did I know about brains and the physical effect of slipping? All I knew was that I did it and it typically sucked big time.

"So what did you do after you noticed this?"

"We did CT scans every chance we could, sometimes we would catch a slip, sometimes not, but being able to see one beginning and telling her when it started made her subconsciously, then consciously, notice a slip. After that, learning to control it was trial and error on her part. I'm still unsure how she does it but she is good at it. Although she does still occasionally accidentally slip unaware, for the most part, she has it under control."

"Can you teach me?" I felt a ray of hope and tried to put it out.

"That is what we are going to do today, but without the use of the CT machine don't get too hopeful. Robert has been trying with marginal success though. Even if you can do it once-"

"Even if I can do it once maybe I can get more info on Kara and give her some hope so, let's get started!"

"Okay Miranda, I need you to relax and focus. We are going to work on some techniques I have been trying on Robert." I laid back on the couch at Bill's direction and closed my eyes.

* * *

Robert sat behind his father's desk and watched the two of them. She was at ease, and once again he marveled at the change in her personality when she was with him or anyone else who knew about her. She was normal. No, that was not right. She was better than normal. She was witty, smart, sweet, and caring. She could cut him to the core with a glance when they were alone. Which made it all the more infuriating when he saw her put on a mask at school.

* * *

"Okay, Miranda let's try this: picture a long hallway. Do you see it?" Bill sat right by me and murmured in hushed tones. He already turned on a box fan to drown out all other noises in the house.

"Yes, a long hall."

"Okay, now slowly walk down the hall. The further you get down the hall the deeper you fall. Are you relaxed?"

Nope, I thought and sat up. "I learned how to self-hypnotize at age three. My Dad is a psychologist and helped me control my tantrums that way. How about I get myself to the point where I am pliable?" I hoped he would not be offended, but there was no way his hallway hypnotism was going to work on me.

"Sure, what do you need from me."

"You and Robert should leave the room for about thirty minutes then come back and tell me exactly what you need me to do to slip into Kara."

When Bill and Robert returned a half-hour later I barely registered them. "Miranda?" Bill knelt by my side.

"Yes?"

"I need you to find the spot in your mind that controls how you fall asleep, I have a theory that slipping is like narcolepsy. I'll explain when you're alert. Find a way to recognize the part of your brain that allows you to fall asleep and you will also find the part that allows you to slip."

I listened to his even voice and tried to find what he was talking about. I wasn't sure what I was doing but followed my intuition, and deeper and deeper I wandered in my mind. I pictured what I thought my brain looked like and imagined myself controlling each part.

"Miranda. Miranda honey wake up!" Jill gently shook my shoulder, "I need to take you home before dark." I sat up before I was fully awake.

"I'm so sorry! I can't believe I fell asleep. I will try harder next time I promise." I looked around.

"Where is Robert?"

"He and Bill are both gone," Jill said with a sigh. I didn't have to ask what she meant. Later that night I traded with Rachael again. When I found myself in her room I looked around for Robert, thinking that he sent for me. Then I found a note, written in yellow stationery, posted to the mirror in front of me.

Let me help. I can find her but I need to know more. I can do it. - Rachael

As soon as I finished reading it I was back home in my room. I knew Robert would not like this, but if it meant saving Kara it would be worth it

Chapter 18

I talked to Robert that night, the next morning was Saturday and Jules called and invited me to go to the mall. I felt a little guilty because I felt that I should be trying harder to find Kara, but figured a little "retail therapy" would clear my mind and prepare me for the next time I tried to trade intentionally. Besides, I spent the night full of dread over the talk I knew I needed to have with Robert about his sister trading with Kara.

Jules drove at breakneck speeds but it didn't occur to me to worry, so many things didn't matter because of the frequency I left my body. Somehow not always being in control of myself made me not care about certain things. Although I suspected that some people who slipped out of their skin felt exactly the opposite and controlled everything about their environment in an attempt to feel in control. When we arrived at the mall I perked up more than I had in weeks, a day of shopping was exactly what I needed.

Then I opened closed eyes and slid off dark shades, "no freaking way- not now," I mumbled then squinted in bright sunshine, and quietly assessed my surroundings. I was pleased to discover myself on the beach. The waves were rough and loud, the sand hot and soft. I rubbed my feet through it and enjoyed the feeling on my soles as I studied the group of twenty-somethings in the process of getting wasted. I looked down at my host's body and discovered a barely-there black bikini that accented a pair of breasts so pert and large that they had to be man-made. I smirked; my annoyance fading over slipping during retail therapy. After all, who could complain about a day at the beach in a smoking hot body and bathing suit? Just as I was about to slip the designer glasses back on and get up to explore the seaside, a cute guy plopped down on the blanket next to me. I grinned at him.

"I take it 'Jess' has left the building?" he asked. I just smiled blandly, not sure if he meant the obvious.

"Yes, Jess would never smile like that. I'm John, by the way." As he reached out his hand to shake, I noticed the slightest shift, and I knew that 'John' was replaced by another slider.

"I'm Miranda Stone." *John's* eyes widened and he didn't let go of my hand after the shake.

"Robert Mathews. What is a nice girl like you doing in a body like that?" He gave me a bawdy grin, and I decided that John became even more handsome with Robert behind the wheel.

"What are the freaking odds?" I shrieked. Robert could not stop grinning, we both acted like goofy kids but couldn't seem to help ourselves, this was unreal! We stood up and made our way out of the crowd and walked slowly along the shoreline.

"This beats helping my Dad clean out the garage."

"I was shopping at the mall with Jules." We walked at an easy pace staring straight ahead and at the sandy brown waves crashing around our feet. Neither of us seemed to need to look at the other despite the perfection of our host's bodies.

"This is nice." I stared out into the expanse, "it makes me feel both infinite and somehow connected to the rest of the world at the same time. It seems like the ocean goes on forever, yet on the other side is another country, another shoreline with people I have never met staring back at me over the same body of water." Robert reached over and linked his fingers to mine. We walked like that, not quite holding hands until we found a private area. Then we sat side by side in the water and let it rush against the bodies. The silence felt comfortable. For once being together didn't seem like work. I turned to Robert and gazed into his host's eyes searching for him in the depths. When I found him staring back at me just as intently I felt a jolt rock my entire being, without thinking I leaned in to kiss him.

Then I was back at the mall. I tried not to think of the girl in the bikini kissing Robert, I hoped he knew it was not me. But the brick in my stomach was unbearable and I asked Jules to take me home.

* * *

Robert leaned forward and closed his eyes. Instead of receiving a kiss, he got pushed down into the waves. When he came up he was facing a very angry screaming girl.

"You're my Brother! What the hell man, you know the rule about making out in a host's body! Dude, we are twins! Do you know how sick this is?" she ranted and shook her fists at him. Robert could not remember the last time he saw someone so angry. It took an effort not to laugh out loud.

"Calm down, I know why you're mad, but you've got to understand you were hosting someone I know. It was completely random," Robert tried to explain.

"So what were you two doing, taking my body for a ride? Spicing up your dull little lives?" She didn't calm down at his words. He was thinking about how the last thing they needed was more spice, but he just apologized again and sighed with relief when he opened his eyes back at home.

Chapter 19

As each day went by the pressure built. Everyone seemed to need me for something or had some expectation of what I should be. Pressure. Pressure. PRESSURE! I just felt like the world wanted to fall all over me. All I wanted was to be left alone for one day. I felt it in my spine, in my shoulders, the pressure. The pressure of being a good daughter, student, friend, human. It built up more and more each day. I knew I was ready to pop, if one more person who didn't know me, the real me, told me how I should live my life I would explode and the aftermath was bound to be ugly.

On top of it all, the icing on the lopsided cake was Kara. Kara was starving and God knows what else because of my impotence in all of my attempts to save her. My throat stayed tight and I felt like crying most of the time but kept it all hidden. Only Robert and his family knew what I was going through because they were going through it as well. I called Rachael one night and asked her to trade me just so I could spend an evening with the only people on the planet who understood my fears, but I was wearing Rachael as a mask, and even though her family knew it, it felt wrong somehow. Maybe because I enjoyed being her so much.

When I returned home to myself, Rachael left a note taped to my mirror saying thanks and that she enjoyed my body at cheer practice. The note, for some reason, made me break down and cry. I knew I had no choice. I had to do what needed to be done, even if everyone in the Matthews family hated me in the end. Rachael needed to be the one to slip into Kara. I hated myself for it but I was making no progress and Kara didn't have the time to wait. Rachael could control exactly how long she stayed and they could get plenty of info out of Kara. If Robert still disagreed then I was going to have to do it behind his back. The idea didn't sit well with me because I knew how protective he was of his sister.

When I thought of Maggie I knew I may be crossing a line that would be unforgivable. After school, I waited for Robert by his truck. I just came right out with it, "Robert you know we need to let Rachael trade with Kara."

"No."

I got in the passenger seat, "just take me to your house."

"It won't change anything," he started the engine and we made the trip in silence. He called his family to the kitchen when he got home.

"Is everyone here?" he searched their faces. It was not unlikely for one of them to be gone. For once they were all together.

"Miranda is determined to send Rachael to the kidnapper," he stared at me accusingly.

"I can speak for myself, and yes, if that is what it means to save Kara. I care about Rachael and I don't want her to have to experience Kara, but this has got to stop. It has been weeks and she could die at any time," I studied their hands because I had trouble meeting their eyes. I knew I asked for a lot, and they may hate me. Rachael was not just some kid, she spent the past year battling for her life after having invasive brain surgery, and they were very protective. Even though I understood, I still had to ask. I met Jillian's eyes and made myself stand firm. If I was going to ask so much I needed to act like an adult.

"I agree with Miranda," Bill said softly. "I don't like it, but she is right, and we should have done it sooner."

I looked up at Robert and held his gaze despite the anger burning there.

"I won't let you," there was venom in Robert's voice that made me flinch.

Bill stepped forward and put his arms around his daughter, "we have always encouraged you children to make your own choices. Rachael, what do you think?"

"I have been trying to convince Robert for days. It may already be too late, but I want to help the little girl," she looked as determined as her brother.

Bill turned to his son, "I'm sorry Robert but she has made up her mind."

Robert didn't say another word, but he shot me a glare, then stormed out of the house slamming the door with such force that he broke the jam.

Bill sighed, then said, "I see no point in waiting. Honey, are you sure?"

"I'll be right back, Daddy." Rachael smiled but I could see that she was afraid. She closed her eyes and when she opened them she started speaking in a monotone voice, "My name is Karen Ann Roth, my parents call me Kara, I am nine, I am kidnapped. I don't know where I am or who took me. My name is Kara."

"Kara, we are here to help you," Bill said gently and Rachael's eyes grew wide. She started to cry.

"Please, please help me I just want to go home."

I held her hand and pet it softly, "do you know the man who has you, Kara?" I heard Robert come back into the room behind me.

"No, I never met him before. He does not do anything to me, he just looks at me sometimes, and throws food at me when I'm good." She started crying again.

"Okay, that is okay."

Jillian was crying now, "just try to notice anything you can, any little detail that might show where you are. Okay honey? We will get you out of this."

Kara didn't have time to reply before Rachael returned. "Mama!" She jumped into her mom's arms. Robert closed in on his sister.

"You're not doing this again," he held her, then turned to Bill, "Dad you're a doctor, you know how undue stress can hurt her when she is in remission. She is not doing this again," he stood stared at everyone in the room for a moment to see if anyone argued, then he turned and went upstairs.

"Honey, what happened when you were Kara?" Bill asked softly.

"It was not so bad really, just scary. I was in a tiny room, a closet I think. When I realized I could get no information from my surroundings I started to beat on the door. A man opened it and just stared at me. After a moment he said, Sophie, then we just stared at each other. For some reason, I got scared and came back. I'm so sorry, I didn't even mean to. I really do want to help her."

"Do you remember what he looked like?" I asked.

"Well it was dark in the room, and his face was shadowed, but he was tall, taller than Daddy. He was wearing a blue shirt like the guy who fixes our car."

"A mechanics uniform?" Bill wrote down the information.

"Rachael you may have just saved Kara, and I agree with Robert, we can't have you going through this again," Bill said firmly.

"But Daddy, I can save her!" she started crying.

"No, when you are stressed your body releases certain hormones as a reaction. Kara being inside you in her panicked state can send your body's systems into overdrive. I can't risk that."

"But you will just let Kara die?" Rachael was getting worked up.

"No, honey you got enough information today. Trust me, you may have already saved her." She seemed to calm down a bit at her dad's words, I kissed her on the cheek and said goodnight to Bill and Jillian before seeing myself out. I didn't even consider talking to Robert, I knew I crossed a line with him. As much as I hated losing his trust, I had to put saving Kara before his feelings.

Chapter 20

We finally had a lead on the kidnapper, and I didn't want to face Robert anyways so I played sick from school. I hid my Mom's keys to the SUV so she had to get a ride with Dad and when I had the house to myself I searched all the local mechanics and made a list with my phone. I felt very confident that I would recognize the man if I saw his face.

I got the oil changed at one place, the tires balanced and rotated at the next, then bought a whole new set of tires at the third, all on Daddy's credit card that he kept in the car for emergencies. I planned on telling my parents that I was trying to prove how responsible I could be with a car when they noticed the bill. I could justify the lie if it led me to Kara. There were two more shops in town, but my parents would be getting home soon so I called it a day, feeling defeated. At each place, I searched the face of each employee and didn't think anyone was the right guy. Maybe he didn't work locally, in fact, it would be unlikely, and I felt stupid for a day wasted, yet I still planned to go to the last two places the next day. I fell into bed that night burnt out mentally and physically.

The next day I visited the last two shops in town with no luck or leads. I got home at noon and realized I really needed to walk. I had to let the things racing around my mind ruminate a bit before making a decision. I paced back and forth on my driveway for hours until the sun fell behind the tree line and it became my favorite part of the day. Mom called it "Children's Hour" from the Robert Lewis Stephenson poem and often insisted that Maggie and I play outside during the last bit before the sun disappeared. I complained about living so far from my friends, but I couldn't imagine being anywhere else. I loved my long driveway that was carved into the center of a thick tangle of woods. If we didn't drive it every day I'm sure the trees would quickly swallow the path and block us in.

Maggie was named after those large trees that lined the path and bloomed once a year, although no one ever actually called her Magnolia, except my mom who liked to sing our names to us as if it were a rhyme.

"Miranda and Magnolia, what magic will we make today?" She would wake us up with her songs sometimes when she had something special planned like a picnic by the creek. Me and Maggie loved it when we were little, but I don't think Mom has said her name in over a year.

I continued to pace back and forth over and over as the cicadas and the crickets began to call out to their mates. I absently ran my hand across the Mimosa leaves, pulling them off in rows before letting them flutter to the ground. Then I tried not to think about when I used to pull them off and pour them over Maggie's head. They would make a verdant rain of tiny leaves fluttering down and when they landed in her eyelashes they would always get stuck and she would giggle. I pushed thoughts of her to the locked box I kept them in and tried not to dwell. Like so many things in my life, I pushed the strong emotions away vowing to deal with them at a later date when I could manage them, but the later date had not come yet and the pile of hidden feelings was growing.

Pretty soon I was going to become my own Sara Sylvia Stout and the garbage, one way or another, was going to come pouring out. I could feel it swelling up but I paced back and forth over and over until the sun was long gone, and still, I walked thinking about everything in the world except for what mattered. I didn't think about Robert not speaking to me, or the danger Kara was in, or my parents who were strangers. I didn't let a thought of Maggie reach even the outer edges of my consciousness.

Instead, I thought about the new car my parents promised at graduation, I thought about how I was going to decorate my dorm room in a few months, and how cool my roommate would be. I daydreamed about the most inconsequential things until it became too dark to see the outline of the drive anymore. Then I reluctantly went inside and fell wearily into bed, falling asleep before any real thought could catch hold. Being the daughter of a psychologist I knew that this was a form of self-hypnotism, and that I was doing it more and more just to cope. Dad called it maladaptive daydreaming. I don't care about the term, all I know is that the only way I could sleep lately was to wear my body completely down and keep my mind occupied with fantasy.

Chapter 21

My cell rang at two in the morning.

"Miranda! She's gone, Rachael ran away," Robert yelled as soon as I answered.

"What do you mean she ran away? Why would she do that?" I sat up and tried to piece together what he was saying. I didn't wake my parents. I crept out the front door after taking the keys off the kitchen counter, then I backed the SUV out of the drive with the lights off. When I got to the Matthews' house every light was on and Jillian was pacing back and forth on the lawn.

"She will come back, I know she will," Jillian whispered into my ear when we hugged. I was at a loss for words.

"You and Rachael have traded so many times, and we have been making some progress in teaching you to trade. We were hoping you would try." Bill led me into the house and I sat on the couch in his office.

"Okay, focus Miranda. Think about how it feels, think about Rachael. Hell, I don't know. Just do it," Robert was pleading with me and I was trying as hard as I could, but I might as well have been trying to fly.

"Son, you're not helping. Go sit with your Mom on the porch." Robert didn't say another word before he left. Without him standing over me I found I could focus more. Then I thought about something Rachael told me the last time we practiced slipping at will.

"I think I need to go to sleep."

"Miranda, I know it is late, but please try to do this. You have traded with her often, and you have trained with her all week."

"No, Rachael told me that she first perfected control by waking up a four a.m., during that time your body is relaxed and you're more focused on what is going on with your brain. I think if I sleep for just a bit I can wake up gently and have more success." Bill handed me a blanket and shut off the light.

"Sleep well, I will wake you up in an hour." I found it surprisingly easy to fall asleep, although I expected to lay there anxiously. Somehow, with Rachael on my mind, I nodded right off.

* * *

Bill sat on the porch with Jillian and Robert. They didn't talk, it was decided that as soon as Miranda woke up and could not slip into Rachael they would call the cops. Every minute of waiting could cost their daughter her life. Yet they had to try to find her on their own first. Jillian worried that Kara's parents made the same mistake. They didn't have to wait an hour before waking Miranda though, she stumbled out into the porch after fifteen minutes.

"Daddy!" Rachael hugged her parents with Miranda's arms.

"Where are you, Rachael?"

"I traded with Kara again tonight, I think she went to find her parents. I'm sorry Daddy but I'm not trading back until I'm ready. We cannot help her but maybe with enough time in my body she will help herself."

They all started yelling at her at once. Robert demanded that she return to her body, then they realized that she was gone.

* * *

I woke up on the porch with everyone yelling at me.

"What happened? I didn't trade with Rachael I traded with Kara, and I have to tell you she is not doing well at all."

"Rachael traded with Kara, she says she is not coming back until Kara finds a way to save herself using Rachael's body."

"Well, how far could she have gotten between bedtime and now? We need to get in the car and start searching the streets." Bill sent me one way, and Robert the other in vehicles, and he set off on foot while Jillian called the cops and waited to see if she came back home. As I slowly drove the streets at one in the morning searching for a girl under the orange glow of the street lights I started to feel off. That is the only way I know to put it. It reminded me of the nightmares I had of searching for Maggie after the accident. These dreams plagued me for the past two years, and now it seemed they were coming to life. I felt as though I was living in the dream. Each street that I turned down and didn't find Rachael, much less Maggie, made me fall deeper and deeper down the rabbit hole. I was calling for Maggie as much as Rachael and I could barely see through my tears. She had to be out there. Why did she leave me?

"Maggie!"

"Rachael? Maggie?" I knew I was losing my mind calling out the window for my dead sister. I knew somewhere deep down I needed to get control of myself but the world was closing in and nothing made enough sense to grasp onto anymore. My chest felt like it was in a vice and I could not catch my breath through my sobs. I finally gave up and pulled the SUV over. I curbed it and climbed out blindly then plopped down on the road to finish crying so I could see enough to drive again. I had to pull myself together enough to find her.

***

Robert found Miranda laying on the concrete about a hundred yards from her parent's SUV.

"Miranda, I found her, she's in the car. She is still switched with Kara, but we have her body back. Come on."

She would not hear him. She sat up, looked straight at him without seeing him at all then screamed, "Maggie!" Then she passed out, doing a nose dive straight into the concrete. Robert felt a chill go down his spine but stayed by her side as he called his Dad who came and took Rachael home in Robert's truck and helped load Miranda into her parent's SUV.

"What happened?" Bill asked after buckling Miranda in the back seat.

"I don't know. She was screaming for Maggie. Who's Maggie?"

"I assumed she told you, son. Her family had a bad wreck about three years ago, they lost their other daughter, Miranda's little sister Magnolia. Miranda was fourteen at the time." Robert felt like an ass. Why didn't she tell him?

"I'll call her parents and tell them she came over to help search for Rachael, you take her to the ER. Let me get your sister settled with Mom and talk to the cops, then I will meet you there."

Chapter 22

I woke up to the beeping and scurrying of a busy ER and my parents standing by my bed.

"Why am I here?" I tried to sit up.

"Honey, just lay down," Mom gently pushed me back down.

"

What happened?"

"You should have told us you were going to help the Matthews. Honey, we would have helped look for that little girl," Mom interrupted before Dad could speak again. She looked tired underneath her thick concealer but smiled brightly when the ER doctor walked in.

"Well you're going to have some pain on your face for a week or so, but it should not scar. Use vitamin E oil when you can tolerate touching it, and Neosporin until then."

"How did I get here?" I asked again.

"You fell on a curb looking for that little girl, you're so brave, honey!" Mom gushed at me and shot Dad a look that shushed whatever he may have said. The Doctor told my parents about the antibiotics and painkillers he prescribed for the wound, then rushed off to the next ER patient.

"Where is Robert?" I asked after Mom signed the release forms.

"He went home shortly after we arrived. Let's get you home to rest baby." The ride home was silent, and I tried not to think about why none of Robert's family stayed to see that I was going to be alright. I couldn't remember getting hurt, but I was happy to hear that Rachael was home, or at least her body was. I fell into bed at six that morning, pushing all thoughts of Robert, Rachael, Kara, and everything else out of my mind for the next ten hours. I had disjointed dreams about me and Maggie playing in the yard under the big oak tree that our dad framed with a sandbox for us. I dreamed we were slipping back and forth, then of me dying in a car crash and Maggie living alone in our room. When I woke up sobbing Mom was there to give me my meds and shush me back to sleep.

Chapter 23

Robert tried to stay with Miranda but her parents insisted that he go home. When he tried to explain to them that she didn't simply fall, that she seemed to have some sort of breakdown, they politely sent him on his way with no reaction. After being told several times to go on home that they had things under control, he made it clear he was staying. At that point they just ignored him. Around five that morning he slipped into someone else when he returned to his body he found himself at a restaurant eating an omelet for breakfast.

When returned to the hospital Miranda was gone. He called the next day, but her parents told him she was asleep and then unplugged the phone. All through the weekend, the phone was unplugged and her cell just went to voice mail. Monday morning she still was not at school. His guilt was growing.

He kept vigil by Rachael's side, explaining to Kara that she needed to trade back. Kara was apologetic but told Rachael's family that she had no control over it. The first thing they did the evening Rachael made the switch was call Kara's parents. They came and stayed in the guest room to be close to their daughter for as long they could. The whole situation seemed insane to Robert and he only wanted his sister back and safe.

His anger at Miranda and his family faded as he talked to Kara, but after the anger was gone all he had was worry. Worry for Rachael. Nonstop worry that Kara's body may die with Rachael in it. What would that mean for everyone? Would Kara be stuck in Rachael?

The thought of never talking to his actual sister again made him sick to his stomach. He sat at the dinner table watching Kara's family dote on every word that came out of Rachael's mouth. He noticed the lines forming around his mother's face as she served dinner and tried to smile but could not make it reach her eyes. Where was Rachael? Robert didn't know how much more time they could all go on like this.

Chapter 24

I spent the week in bed and in a fog. Any time I woke up my Mom would give me some soup and medicine. Then I would fall back asleep. She never stayed in the room any longer than she had to. She would just deliver the soup and see me take my antibiotics and whatever else they had me on. I didn't care. Maybe I should have, but it was so nice not to care just to sleep. And the dreams were nice when I had them. Sleeping was nice.

* * *

By Friday Rachael only returned to her body once, and the detectives were no closer to finding the man through the mechanic uniform tip. Robert called Miranda several times a day but was put off by her parents. He had enough. If she didn't want to talk to him, she was going to tell him to his face. He drove to her house after checking to make sure Rachael was still Kara. As he knocked on the door he rehearsed what he was going to say when she came out, but all Miranda's parents would tell him was that she was sleeping.

He left and drove the dirt roads around her house for an hour. He slowly roamed the rural dirt tracks and thought about how crazy things had become. He stopped when he noticed something stretched across the road. When he got out of his car he discovered it was a Diamondback Rattlesnake. He stared in wonder at the monster soaking in the sun. After a bit, he shooed it away from the dusty road with a long stick. He knew most people would just as soon shoot a rattlesnake as see it, but he could not even remember the last time he saw a diamondback. Timber rattlers sure, but Diamondbacks were a rare find. He always shooed snakes off the road regardless of the kind, all they wanted to do was sun and he saw trucks in front of him swerve to kill a sunbathing animal before. It made him disgusted sometimes, but he didn't mind roving the back roads on lazy days and saving the ones he could. After driving around a while more he returned to Miranda's house.

"Mrs. Stone, ask her just to talk for a moment. Please, I just want to let her know I'm not upset with her," Robert hated pleading but there was no way she was still asleep at four o'clock on a Friday.

"I will give her the message," Abigail said as she shut the door in his face. Robert dialed Miranda again as he walked towards his car. It went straight to voice mail. Just when he was about to spin out of the driveway his phone rang, it was his dad.

"Son, Rachael came back. She wants to talk to you." Robert started speeding towards his house.

"Hey, Rachael. Please stay this time, you're making Mom sick. Please," Robert's voice wavered. He tried to hold on but he needed his sister to be safe.

"Robert, listen. I have tried slipping into Miranda all week. That was my original plan, to trade with Kara, then with Miranda from Kara. If my plan worked it would put Miranda in Kara at will, through me. Win-win. Except it didn't work because Miranda seems to be offline or something."

"You can do that?" It never even occurred to Robert.

"I was not sure, but yeah. Robert, you need to listen to me right now. There is something wrong with Miranda. She has been blank all week. It is like she is sleeping but it has been every moment I have tried to trade since last weekend. Is she okay? Is she alive? You would tell me if she died right?" Rachael's voice cracked.

"She's fine. I'm at her house now." He spun his truck back around towards Miranda's.

"Did you talk to her?" Rachael demanded.

"No, they would not let me. I tell you what, I'm going to have her call you okay? You just stay right where you are and I will have her call you." When Robert got back to Miranda's he didn't have a plan. But if Miranda was a way to keep his sister happy and out of that closet then there was nothing that would keep her in hiding. He beat on the front door.

"Miranda! Miranda, you can avoid me but at least talk to Rachael, damn it," he yelled into the house when Abigail opened the door.

"You will keep your voice down. She needs her rest." Abigail tried to slam it again but Robert rushed in.

"Miranda Stone! You need to call my sister!" He rushed up the stairs and began opening doors. She was going to face him. He found her in the second room, sound asleep despite his yelling. He turned on the light.

"What have you done to her?" Robert turned to Abigail who stood in the doorway with the phone.

"I am calling 911," she stammered.

"Oh-lady, please do. I'm sure the police would love to hear

about what you people are doing here." He took the water from the nightstand and poured it on Miranda's face, then dialed his home number from his cell phone while she began to stir and Abigail stood in the doorway frozen.

"Dad, I need you to get out to Miranda's house as fast as you can, I think I need your help," he hung up after giving directions.

"Miranda, wake up right now." Robert didn't take his eyes off Abigail. He was not sure what she would do about him, but they seemed to be frozen at the moment staring each other down, waiting for Miranda to wake.

Chapter 25

I woke up in my room with my mother standing in the doorway and Robert by my bed.

"Robert? What are you doing in here?" I sat up and tried to fix my hair but discovered I was soaked.

"Mom, what is going on?"

"Yes, why don't you fill her in, Abigail?"

Mom didn't say anything. I leaned forward and fell back on the bed when I tried to stand. The doorbell rang.

"That is my dad, you might as well let him in because he's not going away."

"What is your dad doing here?" Neither of them seemed to hear me.

"Robert, can we allow Miranda some privacy?" Mom tried to guide him away from me. There seemed to be something that I was not getting and for the life of me I could not understand why they seemed to be having a standoff in my room, but privacy sounded great. In fact, I needed the bathroom.

"Yes please, both of you get out of my room." When they were gone I slowly made my way to the shower and stayed there until the hot water ran out. I just sat under the stream trying to shake the grogginess. Then I took my time and blow-dried my hair, happy to drown out the angry voices in the living room. I picked out an outfit and applied lip gloss. Only then did I feel prepared to join the fuss that was still going on downstairs. The yelling was over, but there was no peace. Robert and his father sat on the couch and my father sat across from them. They seemed to be having an intense conversation. My mother paced nervously around the room until she saw me. Then she called my name too loudly and a hush fell upon the room.

"Miranda! Honey, I'm so glad you are feeling better," she ushered me to the love seat by my dad. I didn't miss the killer looks she was shooting at everyone else.

"What is going on here?" I looked at Robert.

"You've been really sick, so Robert and his father came to visit," Mom squeezed Dad's hand.

"Oh, come on. She is not a preschooler. Miranda, you had a mental breakdown over a week ago, since then instead of dealing with it your parents have kept you sedated." Robert scowled at my parents. He seemed to be daring them to contradict him.

"Mom?"

"Honey," she could not find a lie, so she looked to Dad.

"We did what we had to do to keep you safe, the same thing we did when Maggie passed. We wanted to keep you from hurting," Dad reached out to hold my hand, but I pulled away.

"You tried to keep me safe by doping me up so much that I cannot feel? So I cannot bother you?" I stood up. I didn't know what else to do so I walked out of the room, shutting the door carefully behind me. Then I started walking. I needed to clear my head.

* * *

After Miranda left, Robert and his father continued to argue with her parents about why it was unethical and likely illegal to keep their daughter drugged when things got emotionally tough. Abigail made a case that she already lost one daughter and she didn't want to let the other one suffer when there was an easy solution. Dr. Stone was adamant that as a psychologist he was within his rights to medicate his daughter as he saw fit. That argument would have likely made most people bow down. However, since Robert's Dad was a pediatrician, he was not cowed by Dr. Stone in the least. If anything he was appalled by the lack of ethics. In the end, they agreed to disagree on the morals of the situation and the Stones told Dr. Matthews that they would take Miranda in for a check-up in a month to assure him that she was as healthy as they said.

Robert shook with anger on the drive home, he had to pull over to calm down enough to drive safely. He didn't slip before he pulled into his drive and thanked God that had a chance to talk to his dad alone about the evening while it was still fresh.

"Can you believe the nerve of those people?" Robert paced back and forth in an attempt to calm down before going into Rachael.

"They believe they were doing what is right by their daughter."

"Don't give me that crap, Dad. Dr. Stone is a know it all asshole. That is all there is to it."

"You of all people know that is not all there is to anyone," Bill reasoned.

"Okay, take the higher ground, Dad. But tell me this, when Rachael got sick, you went to ten other pediatricians and oncologists to help her get better, to second guess your diagnoses. That prick thinks he knows it all."

"He is letting me see her in my office next month. That is more than I hoped for going in."

***

I walked until well past dark. I paced around our property and back and forth on the dirt road in front of our house. I didn't want to go far, I needed the repetition of the same walk to calm me, and to let my mind work. I could not find it in me to stay mad at my parents, they were tight-lipped and misguided, but they love me. I could not figure out much as I paced, but I knew that this method I had of coping, pushing things to the back of my mind, and refusing to discuss everything had to come to an end.

Surely my Dad had to know that he could not medicate the pain from Maggie's death out of me. If I could figure out that being bubbly and comedic happy, then snippy and guarded all the time had mental costs, surely he knew that it was time to talk. I knew this was true as I walked and walked, but as the stars came out I still could not bring myself to face them. Finally, when I was sure they were too tired to talk I went inside. Dad was on the couch and Mom was in the shower when I came in.

"Goodnight, Dad," I said. Then made my way up the stairs. I knew I needed to sort things out with my family, but I just could not bring myself to start it. I fell into my bed and despite having spent the last week sleeping I drifted off quickly and didn't wake until they were both gone the next morning.

I spent the day with Robert and his family. My parents seemed happy to avoid me, and I didn't even begin to know how to approach them. Rachael explained her plan to trade with Kara, then with me. For whatever reason, likely the drugs still in my system, I didn't slip night or morning. I worried that I would not be able to but shortly after Rachael went into Kara I found myself in the dark closet.

For once I wasn't afraid. Kara was safe in Rachael's body. Rachael was safe in mine. I could handle hanging out in the closet to give Kara a break. What I forgot though, were the hunger pains and the stench. I could deal. I could deal if it meant that Kara and Rachael were not here. After a while I fell asleep. When I woke up there was a bottle of water and a prepackaged bar of food. I recognized the taste of the meal bars that Dad saved for hiking. At least he seemed to be feeding her more. I dug into the bar barely noticing the lemony taste, and before it was half gone I felt too full to eat anymore. I shoved it into the pocket of Kara's grimy pants. Then started to pace back and forth in the tiny room. Thinking, thinking, pacing, pacing. After a while, I decided that for better or worse the man needed rattled. If something didn't happen soon Kara would waste away anyway. Even with the meal bar, I felt dizzy and weak in her body. I rapped on the wall the "shave and a haircut" beat over and over until I wondered if this plan was just a sign of Kara's brain starving or a sign of my own insanity. I rapped again and again against the wall with little breaks between each repetition. At first, it was to get the man's attention, but then it became soothing. I don't know how long I kept at it but eventually, I started to fall asleep again.

When I woke up I started the beat against the wall immediately as I tried to come up with a better plan. Then I heard it. Boom Boom in response to my Shave and a Haircut. Then again. Again. We knocked back and forth "Shave-and-a-Hair-cut," then, "boom-boom," over and over until Kara's body wore out and I fell asleep. When I woke up Kara's body had been bathed and her hair was still damp. I was tied to a small day bed at each corner, just tight enough that I could not get free but loose enough that I could move a bit. The room was bright white and the light shining through the window hurt my eyes. I had on a Hello Kitty nightgown and didn't want to dwell on the things that could have happened to Kara's body while he changed and bathed her. I didn't feel any soreness, not any more than the hunger pains and weakness I had grown accustomed to. That was a relief, whatever the man wanted with Kara it was not sexual. Not yet at least. The door opened. I tried to take in every detail of the man when he came in. Today he was wearing blue jeans and a gray T-shirt, he didn't have shoes on and he seemed relaxed. I noticed he shaved the beard off, the skin underneath was still pale though.

"Hey baby," he whispered hesitantly. I had no idea what to do, but I knew I had to figure something out.

I gave the biggest smile I could muster and croaked out, "Daddy!"

He rushed across the room and wrapped his arms around Kara's body hugging her torso as her hands and feet pulled against the restraints that tied them to the bed.

"Why am I tied up, Daddy?"

"Baby, if I don't tie you the other girl will run away when you're gone," he started sobbing and rubbing on Kara's ankles and wrists to ease the pressure of the cuffs.

"I'm so sorry Sophie, so sorry," he gulped and tried to get himself together, but seemed to be losing it more and more. He hugged me so tight I thought he would crack a rib.

"I am really hungry, Daddy."

He beamed, "I have all your favorites stocked up! I have been waiting and waiting."

With that, he rushed out of the room and I tried to stifle a scream when he left. The panic grew and grew inside, but I knew he could not be allowed to see it in Kara's eyes or he would never believe I was his Sophie. He came back with sliced apples and a stack of pancakes.

"They are not exactly like Mama made them baby, but I did my best." The man eagerly unlocked the cuffs from my arms and helped me sit up. After propping a stack of pillows behind my back he sat the plate on my lap and watched me eat. I took a small bite of the pancakes, then dipped the fresh apple into the syrup before putting it to my lips. It was just a hunch, but I figured if a little girl ate something on the side of her pancakes she would dip it in the syrup. I was right because he gently set the plate to the side and hugged me again.

"It really is you," he whispered. Then he placed the plate back in my lap and rushed out of the room. While he was gone I tried to eat as much as I could so Kara's body would build strength. He came back with a cup of milk. I greedily drank from it. After I ate as much as I could he cleared the plate and untied my feet so he could escort me to the bathroom. Alone in the bathroom, I searched for a window or a weapon. Finding neither, I used the toilet and walked back out confidently and hugged the man as though I was his Sophie and he was my Daddy. He lifted me up and asked if I wanted to play checkers. He restrained my feet but not my hands and we sat in the bed with a checkerboard between us as though I was simply home sick from school and he was a concerned father.

Then I was back at Robert's house in the back yard sitting next to Rachael.

"Robert she's back!"

He ran out, "Is it you?"

"Yes, and she needs to trade me back, Robert. I'm getting somewhere. He thinks I'm his daughter. His daughter's name is Sophie, and once he started thinking I was her he treated me like his little princess. He has fed Kara's body and she is clean and in a bed. If he thinks Sophie is gone Kara is going to go back in that closet."

"Rachael wanted to check on you. We were all getting worried, no matter which one of you is in there we are worried."

"Well if he believes that Sophie is in Kara, Kara's body is safe. If not-" I didn't finish the sentence. I glanced down and noticed that I was wearing my cheer-leading uniform, "what am I wearing?"

"Yeah, we had to take you home to your parents. But Kara and Rachael have been stuck like glue. She slept over at your house and apparently, they like playing dress-up with your clothes and make-up."

I rolled my eyes and pretended to be annoyed but really I could care less what the girls did as long as neither of them had to be in that closet.

"Are Kara's parents still here?"

"They're inside."

Kara's Mom and Dad were sitting at the table with Kara in Rachael's body between them. To think I thought my life was convoluted before all this started. I was tempted to ask her to leave but I figured she needed to know anything about the man as well.

"Okay, here is what little I could gather, he is a tall man. With dark hair that's speckled with gray, like salt and pepper. His eyes are very blue."

"How could you see his eyes?" Kara asked.

"He lost his daughter somehow. He is looking for her in you. Looking for her to slide into you. Her name is Sophie. I have convinced him that I am his daughter. When he believes she is there he treats Kara's body well, he feeds her, puts her in a comfy bed, and lets her use the bathroom." Kara's parents both held a hand. I hesitated but continued, "For what it is worth I am sure he, he is not um, perverted. I think he is just crazy." Kara's Mom started crying.

"We suspected as much, by what Kara said, but you don't know what that means. Thank you." Her dad squeezed my hand bringing me into the circle, "that is a margin of relief but we still need to get her body back alive." Before I could reply I was back in the dark closet.

Chapter 26

Robert hated sending Rachael home in Miranda's body each night. Even more, he hated Kara being in his sister's body, and most of all he hated the idea of Miranda being with that madman. However, the alternative was for one of the younger girls to be there. Kara already dealt with so much and was so young; it was no option just to send her back. Sending Rachael was out of the question as well. He wished he knew a female law enforcement officer that he could get to go instead, he wished Rachael and his mother could trade, but for whatever reason, it didn't work between family members. The whole situation was crazy, but he was grateful to Miranda for being willing to go and stay in Kara's and therefore Rachael's place. Rachael went to school in Miranda's place each day, and Robert tried to keep an eye on her but Miranda's friends didn't seem to notice a difference. Well, most of them.

There was Derek Sander. He was one of the more tolerable jocks. Until this week Robert thought he was cool. Derek played football like it was nobody's business. The talk was that he had a full-ride defensive scholarship to USF. He treated everyone like people, and Robert noticed him tutoring the freshmen in History. As of this week, Derek seemed to be hanging around Miranda more and more. He didn't know what made him madder, the idea of Derek hitting on his sister, or hitting on Miranda. During the evenings, Robert worked on Miranda's homework with Rachael. Aside from the college math class she was taking for dual enrollment, Rachael seemed to have no trouble with Miranda's courses. Kara was struggling a bit with Rachael's course load, but they also tutored her in the evening and Rachael's teachers were giving her a lot of leeway. After all, she just started recovery from her cancer last month and barely had peach fuzz on her head. Rachael hated taking advantage of their sympathy but at the moment it was necessary. They all had to deal with things that were uncomfortable until they found Kara and all got sorted back into their own lives.

* * *

After waking in the closet my first instinct was to knock out "shave and a haircut" but I resisted. I had an idea. I went to the corner of the closet where Kara used the bathroom and pressed against the wall. Just as I suspected, the drywall gave in just a bit at the bottom where the liquids seeped in. I decided to wait it out before making the man believe I was his Sophie. I leaned on the wall and urinated as high as I could. It was awkward, but maybe, just maybe it would weaken the wall enough to break through it. I could only pee so much but I found a half-full bottle of water. I hated wasting it in case the man didn't buy that Sophie returned and pamper Kara again, but I had to try. I poured the water over the drywall. Then I waited until I was sure that I didn't hear anything in the house. Sometimes I could hear the sound of a TV in another room, sometimes just shuffling and muffled noises of another human's existence. Today was one of those times when it seemed the house was empty. I took the risk of him hearing me and laid down on the floor in front of the wet spot and kicked as hard as I could using my body as leverage. I just dented the wall when I heard a door slam.

The Man was back. I left the wall and huddled in the other corner to sleep. I needed to weaken the wall a bit more before I called out to him. When I woke up I found I could pee again, so I did it all on the wall. I have been in a few awkward positions in my life, slipping into others randomly and all, but this was just gross. After allowing the urine to dry so the man didn't notice the wet spot, I tapped out shave-and-a-haircut against the wall. The man rushed into the closet after fumbling with some locks and pulled me up into his arms. He carried me into the bathroom and ran a bath. He poured bubbles in and allowed the water to fill until they ran over the edge.

"Just like you like it, go ahead and get in. I'll go get your toys." He went to get the toys leaving the door open behind him. I knew that I could make a run for the exit, but somehow I felt it was not the right time. I took off the Hello Kitty nightgown but left the panties on and stepped into the tub. When he returned he handed me a bunch of my little pony dolls and some water crayons.

"There you go. I'm going to get some clean clothes and throw these in the wash." He picked up the gown and looked for the panties.

"Stand up," he ordered sternly.

I stood up and asked him, "what's wrong Daddy?"

"Oh, Sophie you don't have to be ashamed if you dirtied your underwear, you know we were working through that. Just hand them over and I'll wash them," he held out his hand.

"You have not changed a bit, it's okay baby. Wetting the bed is perfectly normal." I handed him the underwear and he left to wash the load. I sank down into the water with relief. That was close, too close. I needed to make sure I didn't do anything else to make him suspect me. I got lucky because Sophie wet the bed in the past and tried to hide it. If not, then keeping the panties on would have been a dead giveaway that I was not his preschool daughter, completely comfortable with her own dad. I quickly sat up in the bath the way a little girl would and started playing with the ponies. After my bath, he gently cuffed me to the bed in the bright room. Now it was not only white though, he painted one of the walls yellow, and there was a poster of a big googly-eyed dog beside the bed. We played checkers and ate peanut butter and jelly sandwiches. I drank as much milk and juice as he would give me. After I could not hold it any longer I decided to pretend to be Kara. I knocked over the shoots and ladders game we were playing and struggled against the cuffs.

"Let me go, I want to go!" I screeched. He left the room and returned with a cloth. He held it to my nose, the sickly sweet smell overtook me. I blacked out and woke up in the closet. I went to the wall and peed again. Then huddled in the corner mentally worn down from playing with the man all day, and physically groggy from the chloroform, I fell right asleep. When I woke up there was no light shining under the door but there was a bottle of water. I drank half and poured the other half on the wall after peeing all over the weakening spot. It seemed that the more the spot softened the more my resolve hardened. I was going to get this little girl home.

The next morning I knocked shave-and-a haircut. The man came, ran a bubble bath, and so began another day. He gently brushed the tangled mess out of Kara's hair and then made pancakes for lunch and chicken soup for dinner. I asked him that evening if he remembered when we used to go play in the yard. He beamed and promised to take me outside the next day. Then he begged me not to go. I didn't have to fake the tears but he misunderstood the meaning when I cried in his arms and told him I wish I could always stay. I slept in the bed that night, I felt a little guilty because I knew I needed to keep working at the wall but I fell asleep without pretending to slip first. When I woke up at dawn I had to pee. So I screamed and banged on the wall until the Man put me into the room. He was so tired he did not even bother with the chloroform. After I heard the locks on the door I promptly peed on the wall, then went back to sleep in the corner. I worked on wetting the wall all day. The Man came a few times and checked on me searching Kara's face for a trace of his daughter, but I just cowered in the corner each time. When he dropped a bottle of water in the room I used the cap to push into the wall where I softened it, then I poured the whole bottle into the hole. Then I knew it was time for Sophie to return. I knocked and knocked but he didn't answer. I guess he was gone again. I sat there weighing the options of trying to escape through the softened wall or wait until I knew it would break through.

Then I was at my own house eating dinner.

"Excuse me," I said and left my plate. I went up to my room and called Robert.

"It's Miranda, when Rachael comes back you need to tell her to wet the wall in the corner where there is a little hole each time she is in the closet. She will know what I mean. Did you get any leads on the name Sophie?" I spoke as fast as I could knowing my parents would not tolerate me leaving dinner for long.

"Yes," he answered. Then I was back in the closet. That was a short slip, I wondered why Rachael even bothered. Maybe just to check on me, I guess. I knocked on the wall until The Man let me out.

"Let's play outside," he said and led me by the hand into a small yard with a brand new swing set and a six-foot high chain-length fence with no gates connecting to each corner of the back of the house. I made a note not to leave out the back door when I finally made a run for it. I ran to the swing and yelled to the man, "push me, Daddy!"

He stayed outside pushing me until the sun fully set. Then we went inside and he handcuffed my ankle to the kitchen table while he made dinner. As he shuffled around the kitchen I thought of pretending Sophie was gone but he seemed so content, and the spaghetti sauce he was cooking smelled so good, I could not bring myself to make the day come to an end. I wondered if I was developing Stockholm's Syndrome? We ate dinner then he helped me brush my teeth and left me alone in the bathroom. I double-checked for something to use against him but aside from some toilet paper and little pony dolls it was empty.

"Read me a story?"

He cuffed my ankles and hands to the day bed then he read a children's book to me. I woke up back in the closet. I guess he didn't want to go through the nighttime tantrums again. I wet the wall and went back to sleep. I woke up sometime later and noticed that the house was once again silent, devoid of human sounds. I tried to measure the time it stayed silent. He clearly worked somewhere. It seemed he stayed gone for a certain amount of days and the same amount of time. I think he was counting on me not being the same person, and not being observant of his schedule. I laughed out loud when I realized that we all had one big advantage in that sense. The only thing that kept me sane was when I slipped. It didn't happen as much as I would have liked for my sanity, but it did offer me a break from the closet. Even when I slipped into the most mundane of lives I was grateful for the reprieve. I always called Robert and let him know what I could. Even details like the fact that the man cooked good homemade pasta sauce and recently bought a fence and a swing set. Or that it rained at night, or that I was growing to feel sorry for him. This made Robert angry. I knew he could not understand.

One morning I realized it was time. I had to go. The wall smelled of urine and mildew and caved under my fingers. Sooner or later he would notice this. He was gone to his job or whatever he did and the line under my door indicated that I had some time before he returned. I knocked shave-and-a haircut a few times to be sure, then I started tearing down the drywall. It only took a few moments to get through the first layer into the frame between the walls, I could fit between the boards but I had to get through the next level of drywall. My heart stopped, then I started pounding on it in anger. To my surprise, it gave a little bit. I pushed harder putting all my weight into it, and it gave enough from the bottom that I could push myself through. I guess pushing from the inside out instead of with the nails was easier. I didn't have time to think of why. I had to move. My heart pounded so hard it was all I could hear, but I was pretty sure I was still alone. I made my way to the front door. I was surprised to find that it had a simple lock on it. I guess he never expected Kara to be able to get out of the closet. I opened it and ran down the steps into a short drive. I was in a residential neighborhood. I smiled at this point. I felt so afraid like someone was going to claw at my hair and yank me back at any second. I ran down the road to the neighbor's house as fast as I could. I knew I was taking a risk of him coming home and finding me on the road. The smarter move would be to cut through the woods but I was already halfway there by the time I realized it.

I saw a pick-up truck coming and thought I would pass out, but I kept running. There was a minivan coming from the opposite direction. What did the man drive? I kept running down the road towards the house as fast as Kara's little legs would carry me, but she was out of practice and weak. When the pickup pulled off the road in front of me I turned around. Then the minivan cut me off in that direction. That is when I lost it. I started screaming, and I just ran blindly. Then I was sitting in Robert's living room.

"I need to go back now!"

"Miranda, Rachael wanted to trade to see if you could tell us anything." Robert held my hand.

"She — I was free, but I think he found me. I was on the road running and a truck and a van stopped. What if it was him?" The Matthews and the Roths cheered a bit, but then the room fell somber. What if the man was in the truck? What if he got Kara back? What if he became angry and hurt her? Kara was in Rachael's body and could not trade, we had no way to know what was going on and the fear and stress made the air brittle. Time seemed to stand still. What could we do? We sat for what felt like forever. I felt an odd mixture of complete helplessness and a small hint of hope.

"Robert, she is out. She is going to be okay right?" I knew he didn't know any more than anyone but I needed to hear him say it. He gave me a weak smile and said yeah, but I could tell he could not muster up much of a response. When Carla's cell finally rang we all hung on all of her words.

"Thank you, thank you. Is she okay? Yes, we will meet you there." She wrote down an address and hung up the phone. It was the Broward County Sheriff's Department. Turns out the drivers in both the vehicles I was running from had already called 911 when they saw a dirty little girl running screaming down the street. Neither of them was the kidnapper. The deputies arrived right after the cars were parked. They took Kara to the nearest hospital where the Sheriff's Department would guard her until her parents arrived. It was a six-hour drive from our small town to Broward County. We all left immediately. I called Mom and told her that the Matthews family had an emergency concerning Rachael and I wanted to go and be with Robert. Since the night I awoke to find that they drugged me I rarely saw my parents. Rachael had been in my body during most of the time spent with them, but things seemed okay because Mom didn't argue. Instead, she told me I could use the emergency credit card if I needed to and be safe. I stared at my phone after hanging up and wondered what came over my mother.

Kara remained in Rachael during the trip. We all rode in the Matthews' SUV. Now and then Jill would ask her how she was doing, and she would inform her that she was still Kara. I could tell Jill was beside herself. I stared out the window wishing Rachael would trade back now that Kara was safe. I slipped once on the trip into a student, go figure. I had been missing school a little anyways. It was a middle school history class. I made sure to answer as many questions out loud and take good notes for the girl, to earn her a few brownie points with her teacher. The rest of the trip I spent leaning against the door sleeping. By the time we got to the hospital, it was dusk. We all filed in eagerly to see Kara, or Rachael in Kara's body. I know Carla and Jensen were eager to find out why their daughter still had not traded back, and Kara's Mom just seemed eager to have her daughter in only one place and in her arms. They sent Kara's parents in first. Carla insisted that Rachael go with them, considering that Kara was technically her at the moment it made sense. I saw Jillian start to protest, then she just sank down in the waiting room chair to wait for her turn.

Chapter 27

When Carla and Jensen walked into their daughter's hospital room and found her sitting up on the bed they tried not to cry, but the tears came anyway. They hugged her and Rachael at the same time and could not find the words to express the relief that finally came. The words were not needed though, for the first time in a long time Kara felt at home even though she was in a hospital room miles from normal.

After the tears dried Jensen said, "okay, Rachael you can trade back now." He looked from one girl to the other.

"I need my Mom," she said from Kara's mouth. When Jillian got there she looked between the two girls.

"What is going on?"

"I can't get back Mama, I have been trying and trying but I can't get back!"

"Give it some time sweetie. I am sure you will slip soon enough. Just calm down," Jillian tried to soothe her daughter but it was clear that she was shaken as well. What if suddenly Rachael was static?

* * *

We stayed in the hospital overnight and they released Kara that morning. After breakfast at IHOP, we drove home. The relief of having Kara safe was huge. A weight had been lifted from all of us. Kara's parents looked better than I had ever seen them, but we were all a bit subdued. The complete relief didn't take away the very sensitive issue of Rachael and Kara being stuck in each other's places. I laid my head on Robert's shoulder and drifted off to sleep. Maybe they would trade back by the time I woke up.

I slipped in my sleep into another family driving in a vehicle. I laughed out loud, I couldn't help it. When the mother asked me what I found amusing I explained that I came from another car on a seven-hour trip, and just slipped into the same situation. The whole family found humor in the trade and couldn't wait to tease their daughter when she returned. Slipping during a long trip could be a treat to break the monotony, but sometimes things just happen like that. I didn't return to my own body until late that night. I woke up in my bed and instantly called Robert.

"Are things back to normal?"

"No. Kara's family is staying here until things get sorted out," Robert sounded weary and I found myself wanting to reach out to him.

"It will work out. I promise. This is better than where we were last week," I didn't know what else to say.

"I know, I know. I just wish she didn't feel the need to save everyone. I have never seen anything like this, Miranda. We're scared for them both," Robert sighed. "Are you coming to school tomorrow?"

"Yeah, everyone thinks we should just live like normal."

"I'll see you in the morning then," I told him then hung up.

In the morning Robert met me when I got off the bus.

"Miranda, there is something I haven't told you," he looked nervous.

"Don't worry, I don't care if Rachael didn't want to hang out with my friends and stuck by you. They will get over it." Robert looked pained, "no that is not it."

"Well, what is it?" Before Robert could answer Derek Sander came up to us and grabbed my hand. I tried to pull it away but he grinned and pulled me into him with a hug. I looked over his shoulders at Robert but he just shrugged looking miserable. Derek and I had been friends for years, but I never saw him as anything more. In fact, I never thought too much about him either way, but when Rachael was in my body she clearly didn't feel the same.

"Derek."

"Miranda, I called you all weekend. Your mom said you and Robert had a family emergency?" I looked at Robert again, lost completely.

"Yes, our cousin Kara was in the hospital. So glad our little cousin is better right, Miranda."

"Our cousin?" I asked, truly baffled. Then I slipped. By the time I returned, it was lunch and I was sitting between Derek and Shannon. I looked around for Robert but could not find him. I unraveled my hand from Derek and went to the senior parking lot to find Robert. I got there just as he was pulling in.

"I see you adjusted to your new boyfriend easily." He leaned against the side of his pick-up and tried to look casual but I could see the fire in his eyes. In fact, his whole attitude was pretty transparent to me now that I knew him.

"Yeah, I have not even been here. She is your sister, do you think maybe you could have stopped her from using my body to date?"

"I didn't know about it until they-y'all were already an item. What could I do, no one would believe that it was my little sister in you."

I rolled my eyes. "That does not explain you making out with him between every period today and at lunch."

"Robert, I spent all day, up until about ten minutes ago, doing paperwork in some law firm. As soon as I was me again I came straight out here. Apparently whoever traded with me felt like it would be my normal behavior, or maybe she has a thing for cute jocks."

"Maybe you do," Robert's eyes were still heated but I could tell he was calming down.

"Let's go."

"What?"

"Come on *cousin*. Let's blow off the rest of the day," I hopped into the passenger door of his truck and then quickly cleared the distance between us on the bench seat. When I noticed the tension ease from his shoulders at my suggestion my heart melted. He started the Chevy and pulled out of the parking spot. I put my hand on his knee and scooted closer. Even if we just went home to hang out with his family we both needed downtime. It had been a horrible few months, and until Rachael and Kara traded back it would not be over. For the moment though, we could both pretend to just be two kids playing hooky. I grinned up at him, hoping he might lean down and kiss me, but all I saw was confusion in his eyes. The slider hid it fast and asked casually where we were going again. I sighed, unable to hide my disappointment.

"We were just getting back from lunch. Park wherever. Your next period is Economics room 302." I got out of the car and spent the rest of the day at school like I was meant to. I knew I was going to have to break it off with Derek, and I needed to have a long chat with Rachael about the mess she made of it all, but that evening after I called to check on her I took to pacing my driveway and yard instead pursuing the issue.

Chapter 28

Once again Robert found himself gone into another life as soon as Miranda started opening up to him. It didn't fill him with anger though, as much as he would have loved to spend the afternoon with her he knew she would be there when he got back. She was becoming someone he could depend on. He tried not to dwell on the image of her and Derek kissing in the hall and leaning all over each other. It was a hell day watching them, even if he knew chances were good that it was not Miranda at all. The tension in his body didn't ease even after she confirmed that she had slipped all day.

That evening he tried calling her, but she didn't answer her cell. His dad told him she called to check on Rachael about an hour ago, and that was it. Rachael and Kara continued to be stuck. There was not much he could do about it so he just hung out with them all and wondered why Miranda withdrew into herself today. He searched in the kitchen through all the papers gathered there that had to do with the research done on the kidnapper. Miranda had taken to calling him The Man, and she seemed to have a sympathy for him that annoyed Robert. The police called that morning and told Kara's parents his identity. Conner. Conner Adams. Somehow Robert thought putting a name on the man would make him less horrible, but even after an internet search discovering his back history, and studying his picture he still seemed just as evil as before. There was no denying the tragedy of a person losing his entire family in a car accident, it was senseless. But to reach out and hurt a little girl, nothing could justify that. As far as Robert was concerned, there was no excuse for what he did. He printed out the picture and news story and drove over to Miranda's house.

* * *

Robert pulled into my driveway just as I was getting good momentum to my pacing. I had intentionally left my phone inside because I needed to be alone. Still, I didn't mind a bit when he stopped beside me.

"Will you get in, there is something I want to show you?"

"Sure," I climbed into his truck and moved the folder he had on the seat next to him out of the way so I could sit close as possible. He smirked, but leaned across me and pulled the folder onto my lap.

"The cops called today. The house Kara identified belongs to a man named Conner Adams. He was a cop in South Florida until his wife and daughters were killed in a car accident. After that he went crazy, yelling at people, mainly women. He would tell them that he knew them, and he would call out his wife's name or his daughter's name to strangers on the street. As if the strangers somehow had his family trapped inside them." Robert looked at me, waiting for a comment I guess, but I just studied the man's face. He was sitting on a porch swing next to a lovely redhead. He had two young girls, about six and four years old on each of his knees. He seemed so normal, so happy. The image of his face as he slammed the closet door in my face came to the forefront and I got chills. Robert put his arms around me.

"I never told you thank you for saving Kara and my sister. None of us did, I guess it all happened so fast, and now with the mix-up between the two no one has stopped to ask how you're coping."

"Kara's parents have called me a few times, and your dad tried to set me up an appointment with the same post-traumatic stress specialist that Kara and Rachael are seeing. He's like us, and your dad thinks he could help, but I don't want that. I just want to forget about it."

"Like you did with your sister?" Robert asked.

"Yes-no. This is not the same." I scooted away from him.

"I'm not trying to attack you, Miranda. You have dealt with a lot, and your parents have not exactly taught you the proper way to cope, to grieve. Not to mention having to hide such a big part of who you are from them, but it's time to find a new way." Robert held my hand and tried to pull me back to his side. Even though I knew every word he said was right, it was easier to pretend I didn't, to get mad and sulk, than to deal. I put my hand on the door handle.

"Miranda." I pulled my hand away, but I could not look at him.

"Her name was Maggie. We were Irish twins, born ten months apart. We did everything together and we didn't need anyone else. She was the only one who knew about me leaving myself. Then she died. She died in a car accident and I was not even there. I was gone into some kid at the movies. I don't even remember the movie." I didn't know what else to say, I never talked about her before. It was simply not done in my family. Robert pulled me to him and leaning into his shoulder

I finally cried. I cried for Maggie, for myself and my parents, for Rachael and Kara, and even for Conner and his girls. It seemed that once I started I couldn't stop but Robert just sat there letting me leak all over him. When I finally dried up he handed me an old fast-food napkin to wipe my face with.

"Well that was lovely," I said. Then we both burst out laughing.

"So what do you do when you walk your drive?"

"I dunno, I just pace and think about things. Sometimes really shallow things like what kind of car I want, sometimes I think of Maggie and how we used to build our forts in the trees lining the walk. It is just my alone place." We got out of the truck.

"Can I join you today?" Robert took my hand and we walked back and forth until sunset.

Chapter 29

They took her. The bastards took his Sophie, she was the only one he managed to get back after all these years, and now she was gone! He sobbed as he drove ignoring the small form in the back seat struggling against the ropes she was tied in. He would get Sophie back though. For now, he had to leave, to continue to put distance between himself and Florida, and head to his bug-out shelter. Someplace where his picture was not splattered all over the news.

He got out of town the second he saw the police lights on his road. He had his bug-out bag already packed in the back of his SUV. The time came to stop lamenting over losing the girl who held Sophie in her. Stop thinking about how much Sophie would have liked this new girl, the one who held her sister Grace. He just had to cut his losses and go into hiding for a while.

"One day. One day, all my girls will be together again," he vowed to the girl in the back seat, "you just wait, sooner or later we will all be together."

Chapter 30

The next day I knew I had to confront my parents. Things were all sorts of screwed up with Rachael and Kara. I had a boyfriend I barely knew that I had to break up with. And Robert – Robert was becoming a good friend, the best I had since Maggie. I finally had someone I could be myself with. Maybe that is what gave me the strength. Maybe just seeing what could be lost when I looked at Rachael and Kara gave me courage. I don't know why but I knew today was the day. So at breakfast, I just went for it.

"I know you guys adopted me," I said and then I took a sip of my orange juice.

"Miranda," Dad seemed to be building up to a lecture, then he sat down his fork and just stared at me. Was he finally at a loss for words?

"Dad, I just wanted to let you know that I know. It doesn't seem healthy for me to keep it inside so let's just get it out." I searched the room for courage but found none. I went on anyways, "Maggie, she was yours though. Wasn't she?" I studied my plate and tried to hold it together.

"You were ours too," Mom stood up.

"NO! No more lies Mom. I know okay? I know I was adopted, I know your real daughter died and you wish it were me. I do too. I wish it was me too." Damn, it! I was not going to cry in front of them. Mom put her arms around me.

"Miranda, I wasn't lying. You were and you are ours as much as Maggie. Yes, you were adopted but I swear I didn't love you one little bit less than her. Look at me, Miranda." I forced my head out of my hands. Why was this so hard? I looked at my Mom. It was Sunday morning and she had her makeup on and hair done for church, but it was all messed up now. She was crying as hard as me. Dad knelt beside my chair as well.

"Miranda, your mom and I could not have a baby. We tried and tried for years then we were blessed with you. We adopted you through our church when another family, your Mom, Dad, and older brother died in an accident. You were our joy and our miracle for two reasons. First, because we loved you so much, and then because Mom found out she was pregnant with Maggie when you were with us a month it was like her love for you made Maggie possible after years of trying." Dad looked wistful, Mom reached out and held his hand. I could not remember the last time I saw them touch each other.

Mom continued, "I worried when I was pregnant that it would be different because Maggie was my blood, but I promise you, baby, I love you just as much as her. I never wanted you to be hurt, I would not trade either of my girls."

"I still wish it were me," I mumbled, hating myself for hurting her but wanting to be honest.

"I'm sorry Miranda. I think we all handled losing Maggie all by ourselves instead of as a family. I'm sorry you felt alone and unloved. Baby, I'm sorry we made you sleep, sorry we drugged you. The pain was just too much to bear, and I didn't want you to have to deal with it every second like we did. You girls were so close, we worried losing Maggie would kill you." By then we were all crying but we didn't run away. For us that was a miracle. We stayed home from church that morning and Mom told me about my birth family. She even had a box of pictures. The family in the photos appeared young and beautiful but somehow I didn't feel an attachment to them. I felt sad that their lives were cut off but Maggie and the parents who raised me seemed much more real than the parents and brother I never met.

That evening when Derek stopped by I took him out to the lattice gazebo in the front yard.

"I'm sorry, but we need to break up." I came out and said it immediately. I felt nervous. I dated before but never had a steady boyfriend. Now I had to break up with a guy. It seemed unfair to only get this side of the relationship.. "Miranda, you have seemed so different this past week. What happened?" He seemed at a loss. I was just shocked that he noticed Rachael was missing. He must have really liked her.

I decided to be as honest as I could, "I grew up a bit. I guess everything going on with my cousin has put things into perspective."

"Speaking of cousins, you and Robert don't act like any cousins I have ever seen." He was bitter. I didn't mind though, bitter seemed better than angry.

"He's a second cousin and I think you need to leave," I hedged. At this point, I was agitated that he made me have to lie.

Derek stepped closer.

I stepped back.

He put his arm around my waist.

"One goodbye kiss?" Before I could say no his lips were on mine. Just his lips ever so gently pressing against me, then he pulled my hips into his and I felt myself responding. I leaned in a bit enjoying the heat of his mouth. The subtle scent of his aftershave and the pressure of his hand on my back made me enjoy myself, just a little. A horn blared and I jumped back as though I stepped on a cottonmouth snake. I felt about the same rush of adrenaline too. Derek was smirking.

"Bye Miranda, your cousin is here," then he was gone.

Robert stalked up, "Well, that was nice to see."

"I just dumped him."

"I could tell."

"He kissed me."

"He was being kissed too." I was mortified, but I decided to level with him.

"Robert, I think Rachael has, um, well, I think she has trained this body, my body, to really enjoy his body." Robert turned red. I realized being honest was probably not the best route to take.

"So you're trying to make me feel better by saying that my little sister has made out with him so much—with your body—that you instantly get all turned on at his touch? Nice Miranda." He got back in his truck and left me in a cloud of dust.

Sheesh, I finally confront the problem with my parents and a whole new garden of weeds pop up. Then I grinned. I could not help it. As much as I hated making Robert mad, I had to admit that it was nice to have a somewhat normal teen drama. I faced my parents and actually talked to them about issues we buried for years. Now I was dealing with a hot jealous guy and a sulky ex-boyfriend and perhaps a case of lust for both of them. This I could deal with. For the moment I planned to just enjoy the normal

Chapter 31

Aftershocks from the kidnapping still rippled through the family. However, everyone seemed to want life to become a semblance of normal again. Finding out why the girls would not or could not switch back was the purpose of life each day. The girls both tried, but slipping into each other simply didn't happen. Rachael still slipped out of Kara into other hosts, but Kara was not budging from Rachael's body at all. By Saturday evening everyone was at a breaking point.

"This is better than her being in that closet, waiting for a madman to feed her," Miranda pointed out when it seemed that everyone was about to snap.

"No one is saying it is not, Miranda, but this really is pushing all of us. I mean we can't just trade daughters, yet we all have lives to get back to, bills to pay." Jensen ran his hand through his hair as he paced around the living room.

"Dad, why won't you just say what we are all thinking?" Robert sat on the love seat by Kara and Rachael scowling at the group, the words seemed to pain him. Miranda wondered what it could be that everyone was not saying, there was nothing that came to her mind.

"You know Grandma and Grandpa both stopped slipping before they died." Robert was pissed that he was the one who had to point out the obvious.

"Robert-shut up!" Jillian snapped, then added wearily, "I'm going out, I can't just sit here all day." Rachael couldn't find anything to say. She got lost in the what-ifs as she stared out the window. What if Robert was right? What if they were not slipping back because her body was dying? How was she supposed to go on if she had to watch her body die with another girl stuck inside? What would her parents do? Everyone would hate her, but not as much as she would hate herself. She reached out and held her own hand to give Kara some support.

"Daddy, there is another reason right?"

"I'm sure there is, baby." Everyone could tell he was not sure at all.

"Miranda, let's get out of here," Robert glared at his family then stormed out. Rachael knew this could not be happening. Sometimes the only thing that kept her fighting in the past year was knowing what her death would do to Robert. Now so much more was at stake and all she could do was watch herself fade.

* * *

Robert drove too fast towards the coast. I didn't say anything to him though. I understood his rage. I wanted to be reckless too. We didn't speak. I thought about a quote I heard once: 'The test of true friendship lays not in the lack of silence but the comfort in it.' I thought about sharing the sentiment with him but didn't want to break the silence. I laced my hand through his after we parked and we began walking in the sand. After a while, he thanked me for leaving with him. I didn't know what to say, because I could not lie and reassure him that Rachael's body would be okay.

"You know what? I'm glad that it is not Rachael in her dying body. How messed up is that? I'm so selfish that I'm relieved that if the cancer is going to get her body it will not take her soul." He looked torn in two, "but I don't want Kara to die." He sat down in the sand. I settled next to him.

"I worry about Rachael the most if Kara does die with her body. Robert this cannot happen, the guilt that girl will have to carry is unimaginable. It will break her." I started crying despite myself, Robert wrapped his arms around me and we sat on the beach together as the sun set behind us. We were holding on to each other and the hope that it might all work out in the end for everyone. When it was dark we walked back to his truck, words all used up. After Robert started the engine and got the air on I leaned in to kiss him.

I think I took him by surprise but we both seemed to need each other right then. I felt him lift me up and pull me onto his lap. I was pressed against him tightly in the small space but he didn't seem to mind, and I know I didn't. The feeling of him against me was exhilarating. We kissed like that until I thought I might catch on fire. Then I did the only thing I could think at the moment to stop myself from losing my mind in a deserted beach parking lot. I pulled open his door allowing both our bodies to come crashing to the ground. The hard concrete seemed to snap Robert out of the moment, this was good because I was afraid of what I might do if that kiss stretched on any longer or if we sat like that for even a moment more. We made small talk on the way home, and Robert promised to call me Monday afternoon after they took Rachael to see another oncologist.

Chapter 32

Conner knew it was time. It was risky going back into Florida but after the first few weeks, the small-town law enforcement officers let their guard down. As long as he stayed away from the interstates and didn't get pulled over, no one would really look twice at him. If he acted as though he belonged he would be treated like he did. He was trained in the military to blend in, keep cool under pressure, and get his target and return to shelter. He allowed himself to drive by the house twice a day only. Once in the morning, then once again at the same time each evening. The people got used to seeing him, they even waved like he was one of them. It amazed him at how little people looked at each other in the face. He got a small pleasure out of buying his coffee from a clerk who had his wanted poster hanging on the wall behind her head. She called him sweetie every morning and didn't have a clue. He continued to establish himself as a norm and studied the two families that were staying together at the Matthews' residence. It seemed that the Roths were hesitant to bring Kara back home after they took her from him. This suited him well though because he knew the people in her hometown would be on the lookout for him. Here he was just an evening news clip that most of them missed anyway.

Chapter 33

With just five weeks left till graduation I couldn't help but to develop an attitude that was a weird mixture of apathy towards the reputation I fought so hard to maintain, and sentiment for the memories I would be leaving behind in these halls. After all, even if I was not 100% the real me, I was still happy and in control most of the time I spent at school. I was lost in thought about the fact that chances were I would lose contact with each of the people standing in a tight circle around me. Suddenly their chatter didn't seem so shallow. I wondered if I had been so hard on them as a defense? I tried to zone into what they were talking about.

"I think he has a crush!"

"About time someone cracked that nut, but I think he picked the wrong squirrel," Shannon was looking at me expectantly.

"Huh? Yeah, wrong squirrel," I was not sure what she was chattering about but she seemed to find my reaction amusing. I saw Robert walking towards the door at the end of the hall and excused myself to follow after him.

"Maybe she is the squirrel," I heard Jules mock but I did not pay her any mind.

"Robert!" I tried to get his attention before the door shut, but he either didn't hear me or didn't care and he kept going. For all I knew he was not even at the wheel of his body so I gave up and just headed to my next class.

* * *

The oncologist didn't ask why there were four parents and two girls in his office after the cat scan. He would not have asked them anything. If they decided they wanted the entire Jacksonville Jaguar football team in his office at that moment he would comply. Anything to make it somehow better. Moments like this he hated his job. How do you tell a parent that this is the time to say goodbye and come up with a plan for pain management for your child?

After the Matthews' left his office he sat and wondered why they did bring the extra family. Surely it could not be for support, because they fell apart as completely as the Matthews. He tried to shake off the melancholy and not wonder too much about why some people lived while others died. He didn't know why his treatments worked like a miracle until suddenly they didn't. He went home early that day. Some days were not worth it.

* * *

I got the call after school. Robert just said that the doctor confirmed that the cancer was back and had spread everywhere, whatever that means. He said they were going to try to save her but the outlook was not good. Robert choked out the words, then hung up. I conveyed the message to my dad and he said that the oncologist would not give dire news unless he was sure.

I asked to borrow the car to visit the Matthews' but Dad insisted that I stay home because they needed just family around them right now. I didn't have the energy to argue so I paced the drive in a numb haze.

Everything was coming together, then out of nowhere, everything fell apart. I guess it was not out of nowhere though, with the worry over getting Kara back safely from her kidnapper I overlooked Rachael's body growing even thinner. I don't know if Robert noticed it all along. If I was honest with myself, I had to admit that you could see her decline slowly over the last few months. I just could not think about what it might have meant at the time. Now apparently it was too late. I paced until the moon floated slowly over my head and started to sink into the woods on the edge of the property. Dad called me from the porch but I just waved and continued to walk back and forth. I wished I was like Dr. House, I wished there was an aha moment that could solve everything. There was not, so I just paced to numb the pain and feel like I was accomplishing something. My legs felt like rubber but I kept on until I slipped into someone who was sleeping. Then I sat up in their bed and stared at the wall until the sun came up. When I returned to my own body it was asleep. I didn't bother to wake.

Chapter 34

The Matthews and Roths didn't take the news any better than Miranda. How could they? At first, everyone was in shock. The reality set in when Kara could not get Rachael's body out of bed. She claimed she just wanted to sleep, but Rachael knew full well what the girl was going through. She curled up in the bed behind her and clung to her like a spoon until they both fell back asleep that morning.

Everyone walked on eggshells unsure of their role, unsure of what to say. If it were simply Rachael in her own body dying, it would horrible enough, but to have to see another family lose their daughter, while Rachael's body died, while Rachael watched, was surreal and grotesque. Jillian felt waves of guilt every time she dared to feel a surge of gratitude over the fact that her daughter was still unable to switch back. If she was beginning to detest her own self over the whole situation she could only imagine the guilt and self-loathing Rachael must be going through. How was Rachael going to survive watching her body die with another little girl in it? Was there any way her little girl could come out of this sane? Jillian pondered these questions and tried to keep a grasp on her sanity as she did her best to keep everyone comfortable, and fed, and kept busy cleaning every corner of the house.

* * *

That evening I ate at Robert's house. Carla ordered pizza and we all sat around the table. Everything seemed so normal, but so many things were unsaid that I could not bear it. I hugged the girls and made an excuse about homework before ducking out early. Robert followed me.

"Thanks for coming tonight. You make things normal, or at least seem that way," he pulled me to him, and for a moment we just held each other in the drive.

"Will I see you tomorrow?"

"Of course, come by any time," Robert kissed my cheek then I drove away. I don't know how I made it home I could barely see through my tears, but as soon as I parked Mom's SUV I started pacing and praying. I walked back and forth talking to God out loud, I didn't care at that point I looked crazy, and no one saw me here anyway. Every Sunday I sang the songs of worship and I truly love Him. I was taught all my life that he was there for me. So I talked to him, for hours I prayed, and sometimes I even yelled, begging him to spare the girls. Sometimes I felt his comfort, but not his reply. Finally, at around midnight, my phone rang.

"Miranda, we are taking Kara to the hospital. She will not wake up," Robert sounded numb and he hung up promptly.

I tried to pray again but I felt like the world was pulled out from under me and I was just free-floating in space. There was no hope it seemed. Nothing? It was not like I was praying to win the big draw in the Florida Lottery, or for some boy to notice me. I was just a girl, who was not too bad, praying with all her might that a child might live. What kind of God would ignore my pleas? I knew the answer to that. The same God who let

Maggie die, the same God who also took my biological family. My heart grew cold. I still could not deny he made me, that he existed, but I didn't have to speak to him. Not today, maybe never again. I slipped away then, to someone asleep, I forced the body to wake up. I didn't want the peace of sleep, and a part of me hoped when I woke I would be Rachael. I was not, just some girl my age. Oh well, she was just going to have to deal with her body being tired in the morning. When I returned my body was in Dad's office holding a stack of books. Apparently, she could not sleep in my place either. I started replacing the books in the correct order on his shelf. I don't understand why he insisted on keeping his private books in alphabetical order, but I was taught to return them correctly early on.

The last book was a book called *Venture Inward.* I kept it with me when I climbed into my bed. Throughout the night I read about inner body experiences, and how a man could heal himself and other people by venturing inward on an atomic level. It was deep stuff, but it got me thinking and maybe hoping. In the morning I Googled the words self-healing and venturing inward and found a doctor in Big Pine Key who healed people by helping them find the illness within and then helped them kill it. I knew that it was impossible, that the man was likely a quack. But who better to believe the impossible than a girl with no other options, a girl who lived the impossible in different lives every single day?

I didn't wait for sleep, or for the sun to rise. I put the address into my phone, took the gas card and credit card my parents kept for emergencies, left a note, and slowly drove away in my Mom's SUV. I was going to find this man. He was going to save Rachael and Kara. Maybe I was grasping at straws, maybe I was just trying to escape a difficult situation by going on a wild goose hunt. I was not sure but I knew I had to go.

Chapter 35

Robert knew Miranda was at her breaking point, but he just didn't have the emotional energy to be there for her. He didn't leave Rachael/Kara's side if he could at all help it. The families gathered together in a ghastly group to watch their daughters die. It was hopeless, yet every day Robert grasped at ideas of salvation for the girls. Fantasies of a miracle that he knew would not come. When the phone rang a nine that morning, he found out Miranda was gone. He hoped she was safe, but he was almost relieved. It was one less thing to take his attention away from his dying sister's body.

* * *

I slipped when I was halfway to the Keys. The whole time I hoped I would. I left the directions on the dash so whoever took my place would keep me going the right way. I found myself in a pet shop, apparently whoever I traded with had the duty of feeding frozen mice to a wall of reptiles. I cringed and wished I was back in the car with cramped legs. After dropping mice in each cage along the wall a man came in and handed me a Styrofoam cooler.

"Ana, we have a live one. Take her to Bilbo." A man with

frizzy gray hair pushed the cooler into my arms and went to ring up a customer. I started my search for "Bilbo" and unfortunately I found him. His cage was along the back wall, it had a plaque in the front describing him as *Bilbo Baggins a ten-year-old Burmese Python*, I knelt next to the cage and peeked into the cooler. I closed it quickly.

"There is a bunny in there," I squealed and a little boy came to see what I was carrying on about.

"Oh, are you going to feed him? Mom! Come quick she is going to feed Mr. Baggins a bunny." The little boy's mother eagerly made her way across the store. What was wrong with these people? I picked up the little brown bunny and wondered how I was going to live with myself if I opened the cage and sent little foo-foo to his death. I could not just set him free, this was after all Ana's job and I didn't want to ruin her life. Sheesh, slipping sucked most of the time.

"Do you want to pet the bunny?" I asked the boy, trying to buy time.

"Sure," he stroked the bunny for a moment then eyed the snake cage. Oh man, I was not going to get out of this.

"Sorry little guy," I whispered then slowly unlocked the cage with the key I had on the host's wrist. I pushed the cage open with the bunny, then dropped him. As soon as the cage flapped shut I locked it and jumped back.

"You're funny today Ana," the little boy told me without taking his eyes off the cage. I shuffled products around a display case as the boy gasped and his mother squealed. Well, this was the worse slip ever, maybe. I was not sure, maybe it was a tie with being in the closet as Kara.

I slipped back into my own body at nine that evening. Then, I slipped back out and traded with Rachael into Kara's body. I don't know if things were getting too rough for her or if she just wanted to know where I was but I was happy to get a moment with Robert. The Matthews and Roth family were all camped out in the living room around the hospital bed they had brought in for Rachael's body to receive IV fluids and painkillers. I reached out and held Robert's hand. I didn't tell him I was me, it seemed wrong somehow to interrupt the stories of Kara's life her parents were sharing. I thought about telling them where I was heading and about the idea of self-healing, but it also seemed wrong. I kept silent during the entire slip.

When I traded back into my own body I was past Miami at a gas station near the Tamiami Trail. After I filled up and paid, I decided to sleep in the car at this last junction. I was dead on my feet from being awake for forty-eight hours. I know my parents would kill me, but driving was probably a lot more dangerous than sleeping in a gas station parking lot at that point. I woke after just a few hours and continued on. The seven-mile bridge on US 1 at sunrise is breathtaking, the sun glistens on every peak of water and always marks the moment when our family vacations started. Our family would stay at the same little cottage every time we made the long trip to the Keys and we always seemed to finish the last leg of our journey going over this bridge at sunrise. I didn't have time to stop and stare but found it ironic that I would end up on Seven Mile at the same time as we did on our vacations. I hoped my parents would somehow understand all of the things I could not tell them.

I reached the office of Dr. Townsend at eight o'clock sharp. He pulled up in a blue sports car just after I did.

"Are you the man who runs the self-healing website?" I asked as he fumbled with the keys to his office. He was younger than I expected and didn't seem like a professional, but I drove all this way and I was not going to let his youth put me off.

"Yeah, why?"

"I drove from North Florida. My friend is dying, please you have to come." I followed him into the building and continued the speech I planned the entire drive, "she is only fifteen and she has cancer. She cannot die. I know you probably get people asking for your help all the time, but trust me. This girl cannot die."

"Why?" He sat behind a huge oak desk and fiddled with a pen. "Why is she special, when children die all the time."

I decided to level with him, he would not believe me but I had to try, "she is not the one in her body, I know you are not going to believe me, but in her body is another little girl and if her body dies she will have to live knowing this girl died in her place. No one should have that on their shoulders."

"Okay." He stood up and grabbed a big leather bag that I saw doctors carry in movies but never in real life.

"Okay?" I tried to keep up with him as he left the building. He locked the doors behind him and got into the passenger side of my parent's SUV. I had to run to keep up.

"Just okay?" I started the car.

"We need to hurry if what you say is true, you can explain on the way." He put on his seat belt.

"I live ten hours away."

"Drive fast then." I drove as much as I dared over the speed limit until I was off of the islands. After that, I kept up a pace of twenty to thirty over in most areas. I tried not to think about the fact I was nearing a hundred miles per hour at points. Dr. Townsend inexplicably went to sleep before I made it past the first bridge. I kept glancing over at him, wondering if I had made the biggest mistake. He woke up when I stopped for gas north of Miami.

"Can you do what you claim?" I asked.

"We all can, it is just a matter of control." He spoke so casually, but I was on edge. I was worried about Rachael and Kara and I was overtired and ready to pass out. Before I could reply I slipped into someone watching television. I lay on my side on the couch and fell asleep. When I returned to me I was in the passenger seat sound asleep. I startled and sat up, reading signs, worried about where we were. When I saw a sign that said Tampa thirty miles I sat back. Less than three hours till we were there.

"Whomever you hosted didn't know that I was a stranger and asked me to drive. I figured you could use the sleep." He didn't take his eyes off the road.

"Thanks, and thanks for this." I didn't add that I just hoped it worked.

"I couldn't say no could I?"

"How come you didn't ask why when I told you she was not in the right body, do you slide too?" He reached into the back and handed me a fast food bag with a burger and fries.

"No, but I know about your kind. It is funny really that I can heal but I can't slip. You need to eat."

"Why is healing, yet not slipping funny?" I asked.

"I can venture into a body and heal the very atoms, yet I am static. No trading for me." He almost seemed bitter.

"You need to call and warn the Matthews that you are about to bring a stranger into their home. Then call your mother for crying out loud." He handed me my cell phone that I turned off before I left my house to avoid angry phone calls. I dialed the Matthew's number and Robert answered.

"Robert, I need to talk to your dad." He put his father on the line without a reply.

"Hello, Miranda your parents are worried sick about you. This is a selfish thing you have done right now," Bill didn't sound angry, only tired and defeated, my heart broke for the family again.

"I know sir, but if you will give me a minute I will explain why. Have you ever heard of Atomic Healing?"

"What are you talking about, Miranda?"

"I didn't just run away, I had to go to meet this healer who saves lives by going inside them, I had to try-"

"There are a million charlatans out there who will take your money and sell you the moon. I'm sorry you wasted your time but you are not going to waste any more of mine." He hung up the phone. As I sat staring at the cell phone in my lap it occurred to me that the doctor had not set a price.

"Next time let me talk," Dr. Townsend said and I noticed we were going over a hundred miles per hour.

"The Hillsborough Deputies are sticklers for speed, and a ticket will take more time," I told him because my dad had not one but two speeding tickets just from passing through on the way down south. He slowed down just a bit until we cleared the city. By the time we passed Gainesville an hour and a half later, I was on the edge of my seat ready to explode. How was I going to do this? Just march into their house with a stranger and insist on him healing her? I didn't know but I knew he had to have a chance to try.

"So how did you come to know about sliding?" I asked.

"My whole family does it, except for me."

"I thought it is hereditary."

"It is, my healing abilities are how my genes interpreted it though.”

"I thought you said anyone can do it, the healing I mean."

"They can, just like anyone can slide out of their bodies for a moment. Most people just have to try a lot harder than us though," he grinned and then picked up the speed for the last leg of the trip. Aside from gas stops, it seems that I had been watching the world go by at warp speed for the past eight hours. I was going to kiss the ground when I got out of this SUV. We pulled up at the Matthews' at a little past six that evening. I had an army of bees in my stomach as I knocked on the door, but I knew this was a confrontation that could not be avoided. Mrs. Roth answered.

"Hi, this is Dr. Townsend. Dr. Townsend, this is Carla she is Kara's Mom. Kara is the girl in Rachael's body. Rachael's body is dying." She just stared at us for a moment, unsure of what to do. Then she opened the door and let us in.

"She has been sleeping for a while now. Jensen is in the shower and everyone else went for a ride. I'm willing to try anything, but if you make my daughter more uncomfortable in her last days I will kill you." Mr. Roth spoke with such a calm ease that I didn't doubt for a moment she meant every word. I did wonder though if she was talking to me or the doctor.

Dr. Townsend sat down by the hospital bed and held Rachael's hand. She didn't stir. He then laid down on the narrow bed next to her. I looked at Carla but she was just studying her daughter and the doctor curiously. Then Dr. Townsend appeared to simply fall asleep right there next to her.

Chapter 36

Robert saw Miranda parked in the drive, he felt bad for her but she had to know that people preyed on the hurting. It was touching that she was reaching out at anything to save his sister, yet this was taking things too far. When his parents noticed the SUV they rushed to the door.

Carla met them on the porch.

"I know this is your house but I'm going to have to ask you to stay outside or be very quiet and not wake anyone up no matter what you see when you walk in the door." She stood outside the doorway, clearly meaning to physically block anyone from entering.

"Come on, let us in," the Matthews gathered around her expectantly, but she held her ground.

"It is my daughter who will be lost in all of this. I say we let Dr. Townsend try, and Miranda just drove to the bottom of the state and back in less than a day, it seems you guys could do better than to treat her like a leper!"

"Okay, we will not wake her, and we will let the doctor try, as long as it is noninvasive."

Dr. Matthews went to enter his home, but Carla stopped him. "And what about Miranda?"

"We will thank her for trying, although it was misguided,"

Bill had to assure her before he could get past. Robert was not sure what was going on inside, but Carla seemed determined that it continue. What he found when he made it past his family and Miranda was a tall lanky stranger snuggled up, tight as you please, sleeping like a drunk man next to his sister's dying body. He didn't notice that there was the slightest flush of color in her cheeks, color that had not been there in weeks. He didn't notice that her breaths seemed to be deeper, if only slightly. He gave Miranda a look that left her no choice but to follow him outside. He was really going to lay it on her, how dare she subject his family to this pedophilic money-grubbing weirdo at a time like this? He waited for her to reach the end of the drive, then he started yelling.

"You are a piece of work. Do you know that? Did it ever occur to you that maybe, just maybe, the great Miranda Stone might not have all the answers? Do you have any idea what you are doing to the people in there? To the people I love?" he ranted and when she didn't reply he got madder.

"Dammit! Don't just stand there! Go in and get that man away from my sister, I can't do it. You have Carla brainwashed too. Go and get him out and let them deal with this without you." When he saw that the last line strike a cord, he went on, "you don't belong here! In fact, if you didn't get involved we could have focused on Rachael and she would not have traded with Kara, her cancer was in remission before you!" Robert hated himself for the satisfaction he felt when Miranda finally started crying, but he had to get her to get that man out of his house.

Rachael walked up in Kara's body, he knew that he needed to get used to referring to her as just Rachael, but somehow it seemed so wrong.

"Robert, leave her alone," she put her hand on his arm.

"You need to stay out of this one, Rachael." Robert dismissed her.

"I'm Kara."

"This is between me and Miranda. What did you say?" They both turned to face her.

"I am Kara, I just slipped back into my body on the back porch." Robert and Miranda ran into the house. Everyone was just as they left them, watching Rachael and some mad-doctor snuggle. Robert whispered the news to his Dad as not to wake them. Dr. Matthews passed the news on to the rest of the group silently and the Roths rushed to the porch to see their daughter in her form for the first time in months.

Chapter 37

I watched the Roths cling to Kara on the porch and dared to believe that maybe Rachael was healing in her sleep. After all, they said that people stopped slipping right before death. Maybe this was a good sign. I could tell that the Matthews were holding on to this hope as well because they held hands and stood around her bed expectantly. She didn't stir, nor did the man beside her. After a while, we all filed out of the den to talk quietly in the kitchen.

"Who is this man?" they all wanted to know. I went to the car and got the old book that led me to search for someone like him. Then I pulled up Dr. Townsend's website. They were all skeptical still, yet hopeful somehow.

"His family all slip, but he does not. He says that instead of sliding he does this. His spirit, or whatever it is that makes us, goes into other bodies and heals them."

"When will they wake up?" Robert asked me after pacing back out of the den to check again.

"I have no idea."

"Miranda, I called your parents a few hours ago to tell them you were safe here," Jillian said with a hint of disapproval.

To be honest with myself, I was afraid to face them. I knew I needed to, so I said my goodbyes and made them promise to call when there was news. I drove home feeling good about my choice to go across the state, yet nervous about the trouble I was going to be in. When I pulled up the drive I found both my parents waiting on the porch. Jillian called to tell them I was on my way. I sat for a moment to steel myself against the storm then walked up the walkway with my head held high. If I was grounded for a year, I would still do it again to save Rachael.

"Miranda Stone, we were worried sick," my mother held me tight, the same way I saw Kara's mother cling to her on the front porch. I found myself crying and apologizing all at once.

"I just wanted to save my friend and there is a doctor who treats cancer patients and she might die-"

"If you asked we might have brought you ourselves, you can't shut us out anymore, Miranda." Dad led us into the house and made hot cocoa while I told them about the drive, and the doctor, and although I could not tell them about Kara and Rachael finally trading back I did tell them that somehow there were marked signs of improvement.

"Miranda, I read that book. It is an interesting case. I would love it if this works for the Matthews but be prepared for failure honey. Just don't get your hopes too high. I don't want to see you hurt," Dad warned me. Normally his words would put me on the defense but I was just so happy to be home and not in trouble that I smiled and nodded my head. I fell asleep with my cell phone in my hand. In the morning when I woke, they still had not called. I tried to tell myself that no news was good news.

After breakfast, Robert called to tell me that they were both still asleep in the same position, and that they had not moved all night. He promised to call when he had something more to say. I wondered what that meant as I prepared for school. I kept my phone on in classes hoping for a call. When it never came I became more and more nervous. As soon as I got off the bus I asked Mom to drive me to the Matthews' house, she tossed me the keys and told me that if I drove to the Keys in a day then I could probably handle driving across town. My parents really were trying, I felt a twinge of guilt for worrying them. I shook it off and headed over to see Rachael.

When I pulled up I saw Jillian and Carla hugging in the drive. They were not going to stick around to see what happened to Rachael. I could not blame them. They just got their daughter fully back, after all.

"Thank you, Miranda. You saved Kara twice now," Carla whispered as she hugged me. I hugged her and Kara back and we promised to keep in touch. It was one happy ending and I found myself grateful, yet I could not bring myself to say the prayer of thanks. Not when Rachael's life still hung in the balance. I know it may be wrong, but I could not shake the pain that would not let me dare to hope for good news.

After they pulled away we all made our way back inside to sit by the bedside. Before we reached the house Dr. Townsend came down the steps looking a lot older and more tired than he did before he went to sleep next to Rachael a day ago.

"She will need rest, but she should be clean," he said, then staggered back and settled down on the front steps like he meant to. Everyone rushed past him into the house. Rachael was laying in the same position, but her eyes were open and she was looking around groggily.

"Mama? That doctor did it. Didn't he?" Rachael stared at the doorway the man just walked out of. Jillian held her hand and didn't answer. It would appear that he did indeed help somehow. But how and how much? No one dared to say. I stepped out the front door to allow the family their privacy.

"Thank you, Dr. Townsend," I don't know why exactly but I reached out and held his hand. Yesterday he seemed too young to be a doctor and today, even though he looked the same, he seemed ancient.

"I think the Matthews have good insurance, but if they can't pay you I have some savings," I didn't know what else to say so I rambled about money.

"I live on an island in the Florida Keys and cater to rich retirees, I can afford to do some pro-bono work. It does my soul good. Reminds me of when I was young." He had a wistful look on his face and he kept the hand I offered him in his own.

"What was that? Last year when you were young?" I teased him.

"Yeah, something like that." Something in his voice stopped me from pushing it any further.

I spent the afternoon playing chess with Rachael and teasing her about Derek. She blushed bright red when I told her about the situation she caused in the gazebo between Derek, Robert, and I. When Robert walked in we both stopped talking about her love life and I let him take over the game of chess. Things were tense between us, and I knew I would forgive him for his outburst but I didn't want to do it at the moment. I said my goodbyes to the Matthews and Dr. Townsend who was going to stay in the guest room that night. Then I went home to tell my parents about Rachael waking up. It was nice to be able to share the good news with them.

* * *

Robert went with his family to Rachael's oncologist appointment the next day. The doctor could not conceal his surprise when Rachael walked into the office on her own. They did blood work and CT scans but couldn't find a trace of cancer. She was still a little weak from being underweight, but not a trace of illness could be found in her brain or blood. The oncologist was flabbergasted, but it was a good feeling compared to the feeling of hopelessness he had the last time he saw Rachael Matthews.

Robert called Miranda as soon as they left the office. He knew he owed her a huge apology, and beyond that, he would be in debt to her for the rest of his life for saving his sister. He didn't mind the idea of owing Miranda though. He just hoped she would forgive him. Today was too wonderful not to share with her

Chapter 38

I got the call at lunch. I rushed out of the cafeteria and waited at the front of the school. Rachael was cancer-free. It was all too much to believe and I had to see her. The Matthews picked me up on the way home from the oncologist. We were all on cloud nine.

"So did you talk to anyone at school today?" Rachael asked, trying to come off casual. I got the giggles at her question because it was meant to be a coy way of asking about Derek and instead, it sounded completely transparent and typical of a teenage girl. I started laughing and found that I couldn't stop. Robert understood what I found amusing, or maybe he was just on cloud nine because he joined in. Rachael looked back and forth between us for a moment and finally began to giggle. Bill and Jillian stared from the front seat at us and could not help laughing even if they didn't get the joke. By the time we pulled into the drive, we were all laughing so hard we had tears in our eyes, although at this point I don't think any of us could have said why. Sometimes happiness is not subtle, sometimes it knocks you off your feet and makes your eyes leak. The euphoria lasted through the evening.

During dinner, Dr. Townsend explained his process of literally going into a body as his soul and exploring the functions to heal a person. I felt amazed. I know that such a thing should hold less wonder for a slider, but somehow being able to have any control over such a thing seemed impossible to believe. Dr. Townsend explained that anyone could do it, he was sure, but then again he never was able to train himself to slip like the rest of his family. Maybe training for such things was pointless. Maybe it had to be God-given. He was a contradiction, he seemed so young and old at once. He gave a lot of himself to save Rachael and Kara yet didn't want money or praise. He planned to return to curing sunspots on rich residents of the Keys instead of saving the world. I didn't understand him but I found myself attracted to his charisma and hoped he would keep talking through the night. Especially about what he believed was the origin of Sliding. He had a theory that it started as a way for certain people to heal others and themselves, and then a mutation occurred and it turned into people trading bodies. I found his theory fascinating and hated telling him goodbye when the town car he rented to take him home pulled into the drive.

Before I went home Robert apologized about ten times and thanked me about a million, I think. I forgave him at apology number four and told him not to thank me for finding the Atomic Healer, just to thank him. That night I think I fell asleep the second my head hit the pillow. The next morning was Saturday and I slept in. When I woke up, I found my Mom in the yard on her knees working in the garden. I could not help it, I just went to her and put my arms around her. She may not be perfect but she was the only mom I had and after this week I felt grateful for every little thing.

Before I could say anything I slipped to a daycare as the teacher. This was new, typically I was the student, I noticed the daycare teacher seemed to be in her early twenties, so I guess it made sense. I read the kids a book about an Elephant and a Pig who were the best of friends, then I slipped back home. Mom and I were sitting at the table drinking ice-cold tea.

"Thanks for the tea, Mom," I stood to go.

"Miranda, is there something you are not telling me?"

I froze. Of course, there was something I wasn't telling her, there were about a million somethings that I wasn't telling her. "No, why do you ask?"

She studied me for a moment then emptied her ice into the sink, "You will tell me when you're ready I guess."

I paused. I wanted to tell her about me so badly, but how could I? I turned around and hugged her again, "I love you," I whispered. I held her tight and hoped she knew I meant it, even if I could not share everything.

After lunch, I called Robert. As I listened to the phone ring I suddenly felt shy. Things were not high risk now. What would we talk about? All the common problems we shared seemed to be gone, thank God, but it made me feel awkward out of the blue. When he didn't answer I felt a mixture of relief and a twinge of fear that he would want nothing to do with me now that we didn't have someone to save. I shook it off because it was not in me to be a fool for anyone. I decided to put on my sneakers and go for a jog. Then maybe work on a few moves. I let cheer practice and fitness go in the past few months and I was happy that life was simple enough to get to focus on it again. Three miles in I heard the unmistakable sound of the engine of Roberts's old truck.

I didn't want him to see me like this, much less smell me all covered in sweat. What a way to ruin a perfect workout. I considered cutting into the woods before he turned the corner, but my pride kept me on track. I would not run and hide just because I was all sweaty, if he didn't like it he could suck an egg. I stopped jogging as he pulled up next to me.

"Want a ride?"

"Do I look like I want a ride?"

"Actually, yes. You do." He smirked at me from the air-conditioned cab.

"You have ruined the first jog I have been on in months."

"Deal with it." He opened the passenger door from the inside and I climbed in.

"Take me home so I can get a shower."

"You need one."

"Did you come over for a purpose other than ruining my jog and throwing me one-liners?"

"Nope," he deadpanned, then we both burst out laughing. Just like that things were easy again. Somehow, this creep who I was too cool to even speak to a few months ago had become my best friend. I realized how much his friendship mattered at that moment when the tension I was carrying all eased up because I knew we were okay with each other, and that we didn't need an excuse to hang out.

"So Rachael wants me to ask if you can trade her tonight so she can make out with Derek."

"Oh yeah, what do you think of that?" I teased.

"Well until I saw you like this, I was hoping you would let me take you out. Now I don't know-ouch!" I didn't let him finish his sentence before I punched him in the arm.

"I was going to say, I don't know if I can wait!"

Robert took me to the movies that night. Then we kissed on my porch like we were completely normal teenagers. I felt like I could sit on my front porch swing listening to the frogs sing and watching the bats catch bugs under the halogen light kissing and talking with him all night, but at one my parents flashed the porch light so we said goodnight and promised to get together the next day. It would have been a great ending to our story, a possible happily ever after. If only.

Chapter 39

Conner saw Kara the day she left with her parents. He stuck around a few days and watched the other girl. She seemed weak and he could not find a spark of any of his girls in either of them. Going back into Kara's hometown was not an option and he was not sure he was interested in her anymore anyway. He began to set his sights on the older blond teen who visited sometimes. He searched for a spark of one of his girls in her. He looked hard enough that one day he convinced himself he found it. So he started following her. He learned her routines. School, cheer practice, home, and sometimes she hung out with the Matthews boy. He waited for his opportunity and one night as he sat in the moonlight outside her house she offered him the perfect chance.

* * *

I just could not get to sleep after my date. My lips were tingling and my body was ringing. I had to burn some of the energy that boiled through my blood. Since Robert started the date by interrupting my jog, I decided a moonlight run would be ideal. The moon was full and aside from the faint high whistles of the family of flying squirrels that lived on my driveway and the call of a Whippoorwill in the distance, the night was silent. The frogs were sleeping at this time, I guess, and the crickets were done with their mating calls.

I kept a steady pace at first, then got the creeps and sped up. I don't know why I got wigged out because I was used to night jogs. Sometimes in Florida the heat and humidity were so bad the only time to run was in the cool of the night. About two miles from my house I decided that I was going to follow my gut and give in to the fear. I hated turning around but the feeling of being watched was too strong to ignore. Just when I turned into my driveway a figure stepped out of the shadows. Even in the moonlight, I knew the second I saw him exactly who he was.

Chapter 40

onner startled her and planned to use the moment of surprise to chloroform her without a struggle, but when he saw the clear look of recognition on the stranger's face he knew that he finally found his wife.

"Nina," he gasped, then pulled her to him. Miranda punched him in the gut and tried to run away. He held tight though, and within a moment the chloroform he held over her face worked and she went limp in his arms. Carrying her to his car parked a half-mile away was not too difficult because he was on cloud nine. He did not doubt that he found his Nina, and could hardly wait to get her home.

* * *

I woke up slowly. My mouth tasted horrible, and the sun burned my eyes. I was laying on a mattress in the back of a van. I tried the doors but they didn't budge. Then I saw Conner fiddling with the sliding door. He had me locked in from the outside. He tapped a handgun against the glass and smiled knowingly. I backed against the corner but when the door slid open he stood back and I knew that I was expected to get out.

"Well now, who are we today?" Conner asked and studied

my face.

"I'm Miranda Stone. What do you want with me?" I stared right back into his eyes not willing to show fear.

"Last night you were Nina, and I'm willing to wait until she comes back," his voice shook with excitement. I wanted to punch him. Any sympathy that had built up in me for him over the last few months vanished. This man may have suffered a tragic loss, but he also caused as much pain in searching for his family.

"I didn't slip last night, you only saw me."

"Nope, you are lying. I know my wife when I see her." He was so smug, I hated him.

"No, you saw me," I said matching his tone, "and when you thought you had your Sophie, eating pancakes and playing checkers, well, that was all me too." My voice didn't shake and still met his eyes despite the rage I saw building. I guess that is the moment I should have backed down but I could not seem to stop, "I hate to burst your bubble, but you are not going to find your girls in anyone. They are dead. When a slider dies they die just like anyone else. You have wasted your time and-" I didn't see his fist coming at me, but I woke up a while later in back in the van. I sat up and searched for Conner at the windows, I found him pacing back and forth over and over. I'm not sure why I didn't try to play his game this time, but I knew that I just didn't have it in me to pretend to be his daughter or wife. I hated him too much. He changed his path and headed to me when he noticed I was staring. The door was not locked and he slung it open violently.

"Tell me the truth," he roared and the force of his words rattled me a bit but I was not going to give.

"I did!" I yelled back at him just as aggressively. He lifted his hand to punch me again and I realized that his gun was holstered. This was my only chance. I fell to the side and out of the van. Then I hit the ground running. We were surrounded by woods and I hoped I could clear them before he unsheathed his weapon.

* * *

The bitch was lying. She had to be lying, Conner told himself over and over. When he felt her stare he confronted her, but she was crafty, scheming, and evil. Nothing like his girls. It was okay though, even though she got away into the woods it was a game of cat and mouse now, and it all fell in his favor. He was trained to track, and she was just a stupid cheerleader. Conner took his time, he built a fire and ate dinner then filled up his bottle of water from a hand pump and set off to track the girl as though he was searching for a lost puppy.

* * *

Once again I knew I had to run and not stop running. This time I was in my own body and I knew the predator who was after me. I ran as hard and as long as I could, briers tore at my skin and a branch managed to poke straight into my nose. The pain was horrible but I kept running. I try to protect my eyes by closing them often then opening them when I had to. Running, heart-beating, living, breathing, dying. Was I dying? I felt like I must be, but kept on and on. He would never get me back. Conner has had every minute of my life that he was going to get and he would get no more, not even a second. No more of me pretending to be anything to him, no more of catering to his illusions. I ran because he was strong because he was crazy and he had a gun, but if I could have killed him a part of me thinks I would. I ran until I fell to the pine forest floor out of breath and ready to die from exhaustion. Then I got up and walked. I was still out of breath and half-conscious but I walked. I knew he would never get me and surely I would come across a town or a house soon. After all, even though I lived in a rural area in Florida it was still a rather populated state. I didn't think he drove that long, not long enough to reach a wilderness that I could not run out of in a few hours or a day. Despite my reassurances to myself about a city nearby, I didn't find signs of humans other than flattened land where loggers took planted pines. In these areas, there were open rugged fields with a single dirt road edging them. I was not stupid enough to walk the dirt road where he could just run me down with his vehicle. I stayed in the woods following the dirt road hoping for a logging truck or a house.

Hour after hour I walked and ran but still, I never found anything more than woods and empty ugly pine fields. Where were the loggers? Aside from a short prayer of thanks for Rachael's life I had not prayed. Somehow it seemed wrong to outright pray now in my moment of desperation, but I had a prayer in my heart and I was scared out of my mind.

Chapter 41

Robert woke up the next morning with a lightness that he was unaccustomed to. His sister was healthy. Any fool could see the life in her. She was radiant and ready to tackle anything that might come her way. Robert had not seen Rachael so spunky since months before her diagnosis. She was the obnoxious spitfire of a soul Robert loved, and he loved her fiercely. Robert spent the day playing Minecraft with Rachael and planned to spend Sunday evening with Miranda if she would have him.

After their date last night, he was trying to play it cool, but honestly, it took every ounce of willpower to refrain from calling her until three that afternoon. She didn't answer her cell, and after an hour he tried her landline. When Abigail told him that Miranda was not home that morning and they assumed that she was at his house a cold chill ran down his spine and settled into him. He knew something was off.

* * *

Conner followed the clear trail Miranda left. He jogged now and again when the path ahead was completely obvious and paced cautiously when it was vague. He hunted her like she was a wounded deer, his only hope for meat. A pushed-down bundle of grass, a broken tree limb, and a freshly turned mound of dirt all showed Conner clearly where Miranda went. He found a branch broken and damp with her blood and a thread from the snag of her blue t-shirt on another. She was following the road in the shelter of the woods, at a rather fast past. He was surprised at her ingenuity but Conner still didn't rush, she left him bread crumbs and he enjoyed the game.

"Miranda!" he didn't mind giving up his presence to her because maybe she was not herself and not afraid of him. Or maybe he could inspire her to panic and try to run. She was close, he knew it, and now all he had to do was wait for his prey to stir.

* * *

The sun fell fast behind the tree line and the mosquitoes ate me alive a bite at a time. I was sure they were going to kill me before Conner had his chance but I didn't slap them. I knew he was close and I didn't want to give up my location. Then I slipped and I found myself riding in the back of a luxury car. Not a limousine, but I had a driver and was wearing all black, apparently, I was on my way to a funeral.

"Dammit, no!" I screamed. The driver didn't turn to look at me but he raised his eyebrows in sympathy. I guess he thought I was grieving, but I was not. I was scared and angry. I knew that there was nothing worse than slipping right now. I was doomed. The tears I cried at the funeral were genuine.

* * *

"Miranda, honey let's go home," Conner called again. This time she answered.

"Hey! I'm over here, wow it is getting dark," she stepped into the dirt road and Conner put his arms around her. He could tell it was not Nina or Sophie but it wasn't Miranda either and he had to use this to his advantage until she returned. He didn't know how long she would be gone, but if the woman who took her place noticed how tightly he was holding her hand she didn't react.

"What a day huh?" she asked.

"Yeah, I thought we would never find each other," Conner replied and could not help but smirk at her confusion.

"Let's go back to the cabin and make love," he tested her to make sure Miranda was really gone and wondered if maybe she would let him.

"Um, I am feeling stomach-achy right now. Maybe try again later okay?" the parasite in Miranda asked. Conner was disappointed, yet satisfied that she was not Miranda.

"Sure honey, whatever you need," he held her tighter and she didn't react. He was almost giddy waiting for Miranda to return and realize she was caught.

* * *

I returned to my body and found I was back in the van. The stars and the moon were bright and beautiful, for a moment I let myself enjoy the wonder but it didn't last long. I knew I must be far away from any light pollution and therefore far away from any salvation. I sat up and studied the moonlight world around me, a possum was wandering the field, and right next to the van, there was a small one-man tent. I sat in the driver's seat and pressed my feet against the glass in the window. Conner took all the handles out, but surely he didn't take the time to replace the glass.

Chapter 42

Robert did the last thing he thought he would ever do. He asked Rachael to trade with Miranda and go back into the hands of Conner. He hated asking her. He spent the whole afternoon trying to convince Miranda's parents that she didn't just run away again and that they need to call the cops, just to have them brush him off and say that they were giving Miranda room to grow. Whatever that meant. They seemed to like to live with their heads in the sand when it come to their daughter.

He knew that it was in his hands and his parents reluctantly agreed. As soon as she had her parent's blessing Rachael closed her eyes and traded with Miranda. She opened them to discover that Miranda was trying to push against the glass of a van with her feet. She didn't continue Miranda's task because she didn't know her plan. Instead, Rachael studied her surroundings.

* * *

I kept pushing on the window silently with no luck in breaking it. Apparently, it was not going to happen quietly. Just when I was thinking of a way to gain momentum and break the window regardless of the noise, I slipped and was at Robert's dinner table with the entire Matthews family looking at me expectantly.

"Robert, Rachael can't be there."

"I know, we hate it too. Tell me what you know," Jillian said.

"Um, I'm in a van in the woods. There are cleared pine fields and endless forests. Sometimes I went by a creek but the woods are thick and hard to get through, except where there are planted pines. That is all I know. He knocked me out and I don't know how long he drove to get there," I started crying despite myself.

"That sounds a lot like your Rocky Creek hunting lease land," Robert looked at his dad.

"It does, but so do a lot of other woods in the south son," Bill paced the kitchen.

"We will find you, Miranda. Rachael is only supposed to trade for three minutes so we don't have much time but know we will find you." Robert grabbed Rachael's hands and studied me. Then I was back in the van huddled in the corner. Rachael took the safer route of hiding and didn't continue my efforts to break the window. I said a prayer of thanks for her wisdom and got back in position.

* * *

Rachael returned to her body to find Robert holding her hands and peering at her.

"She's in a van with a tent next to it. She was trying to break the window with her feet," Rachael told her family. Robert squeezed her hands and let them go.

"I'm happy you're back," he said. Then he paced with his dad around the kitchen.

"Um, there were woods all around. The sky was bright, the moonlight glowed bright. It made the sand glow where it was worn down through patches of grass," Rachael searched her mind for more information and continued. "The woods didn't look weird, they looked normal but it was dark so they could be across the world and I would not know really, but that was the impression I got. Let me trade again, please."

"No way, Miranda would not even want it. You might mess up any escape she has planned." Robert knew that it was the only warning Rachael would accept. If he simply forbade it for her health she would already be gone.

"You said the white sand stood out in the moonlight," Bill mumbled and continued to pace.

"When I hunt I notice the same thing at Rocky Creek. Robert, you said that Miranda's description reminded you of there as well. I guess it is our only lead." He seemed to be talking to himself, but he snapped out of his mumbling with decisiveness and no one argued when he told them to get ready to go to the hunting camp in south Georgia.

* * *

I laid on the seat and with all of my might, without a care of the sound, I kicked the glass. I was expecting a loud crack and shatter, instead when the window broke there was a dull thump and an almost silent crackling. The glass didn't fall to the ground it stayed stuck in a viscid spider's web, broken but still holding me captive. I didn't move, afraid that even that noise woke Conner. After a moment I started pushing on the window with my hands. The glass gave way easy enough, it tore through my skin when I pushed it to the side but didn't shatter to the ground. I climbed out the window, leaving the glass hanging from the tint like a wound. Once again I was on the run. If I had any luck at all I would not slip. I was not counting on luck though. I knew I was going to have to get me out of this, even though I might not even be the one in my body at all times.

I didn't run helter-skelter this time. I made my way through the woods with care and tried not to make any noise at all. When I felt satisfied that Conner could not hear me, and I would not leave a clear path I ran faster. My mind raced with fear that I would slip away again and be helpless. When a plant jabbed into my leg I knew I had the answer. The Spanish Bayonet is a plant I am familiar with because my Mom used them to frame the entrance to our parking area. She kept the sharp barbs trimmed back in the places they may be brushed against, but there were many times they took my blood growing up. I hated the painful plants as a child. At the moment though, I was thrilled to be jarred by the barb. I plucked three of the pointy stalks and continued to walk. As I went I carved into both my arms in capital letters: RUN. I hoped that if anyone slipped into my life they would take the advice and run from Conner. My arms itched a little from the sting of the cut and the little bit of poison in the plant but the words were big and clear. I just hoped whoever I hosted had gumption. I kept on the same path that I did before. It may have been stupid and easier for him to follow, or maybe it was smart and he would not realize my route. I don't know really but in the dark, it seemed the only thing to do. When I reached the dark creek the woods had a dim glow and I could see enough in front of me that I was not stumbling. The sun had not yet breached the horizon but it was clearly on its way. Somehow this made me feel triumphant, but my celebration was short-lived because I heard a car coming down the dirt road. I ducked under the wooden bridge and stood in the dark water. A fat black snake made its way between my legs and I held back a scream. It didn't seem interested in me though and it slowly went on its way.

The vehicle parked on the bridge and I heard someone get out, just when I was debating ducking under the dark water I slipped.

"Miranda, where are you?" Jillian was sitting in the front seat of the car and Bill was standing on the bridge.

I peered out the window, "I think I'm under this bridge."

Then I was back in my body. I quickly climbed up and called out to Bill and Robert, they were only about twenty feet above me and I thought I would burst I was so happy. Then I slipped again. I was in a small coffee shop. I glanced out the window and saw the iconic marquee that showed that I was in Times Square. It was rare that I slipped into such cool places and under normal circumstances I would be stoked. As it was though, things could not be much worse.

* * *

Robert saw Miranda make her way out from under the small wooden bridge and he started to climb down the incline towards her. When he saw her stop and study him, he knew she must have slipped. She looked down at her arms, then back at him and his family. Then she turned around and ran along the creek edge into the thick woods as if she fear for her life.

"She slipped!" he called to his Mom and Rachael, then he chased after her. He never thought a human could run so fast and wondered what scared the person Miranda hosted so badly that she would react like a wild animal at the sight of him.

Chapter 43

Conner woke shortly after Miranda escaped, and once again began to methodologically hunt her down, he still didn't worry about her being able to get away. This time though, he would shoot her just like he did the other girl. He hated to do it but when a girl didn't work out he didn't have time to wait when she became a hindrance or a wall between him and his daughters. Anything between him and his girls had to go. He found her at Rocky Creek. She was huddled underneath a bridge, he watched as she hid from the Matthews in the car above her, and he saw how close she came to salvation just to run away from it at the last moment. He almost laughed but refrained. Instead, he sat still as a rock and enjoyed the chaos around him. Then slowly, once again, he began to stalk his prey.

Jillian and Rachael were still in the car. They saw Miranda run away then Robert give chase, then Bill run after them both. Jillian considered chasing as well but could not leave Rachael so she just sat and prayed. She didn't expect to see a man suddenly make his way out of the woods on the other side of the bridge and start jogging in the direction that everyone ran off in but she knew what had to happen when he pulled out his gun mid-stride.

"Rachael, trade with Miranda just long enough to get her to go to Robert, and for me to explain to whoever is in her the situation. One minute Rachael, that is all or less. I mean it," Jillian didn't get to finish her directives before Rachael was gone and a panicked stranger looked back at her from her daughter's eyes.

"Don't run from the boy. He is trying to help you. There is a man in military fatigues. Run from him!" Jillian yelled at the girl.

"I think I lost them all." Then she was gone and Rachael was back.

* * *

When I returned to my body I was standing by Robert. Then we started to make our way out of the woods hand in hand. When we reached the creek Bill stopped in his tracks, then picked up the pace again. Robert and I shared a glance, we both knew his Dad traded so we walked ahead and led the way without saying anything. When Robert slipped away a few seconds later I felt very alone again. I told myself it was okay, I still had the company of whoever occupied his body, but his grip on my hand relaxed and after a moment we both let go. They followed my path toward the bridge. When I slipped away whoever was in my place took the bloody words on my arms to heart because we had been walking for ten minutes and still had not reached the wooden bridge. I got a chill and knew that Conner was watching us. I don't know how I knew exactly but I did. I only hoped he would not have the courage to attack me when I was surrounded by others. I didn't have long to wonder though because there was the unmistakable sound of a gunshot and

Robert fell down beside me. I fell to my knees and tried to find where he had been hit when Rachael traded with me.

"Miranda, what happened? Rachael traded with you when she heard the shot, I told her not to. She just did it, what happened?" the words spilled out of Jillian and she looked at me expectantly.

"Robert. I think he shot Robert!" Jillian jumped from the car and ran in the direction of the screaming. I tried to follow after her in Rachael's body, but realized quickly two things; one she was still underweight and could not stand a romp through the wilderness, and Conner was out there somewhere. The last thing we needed was for him to choose Rachael as his next girl. I quickly got back in the car and locked the doors. The car was silent and I felt too alone. I was afraid. More afraid than I had ever been. If Robert died - no I could not even think about that. I felt helpless in Rachael's weak body, the silence was deafening and made me want to scream. When I finally slipped back, Jillian and I were on either side of Robert carrying him towards the car.

"Where is Bill?" I asked.

"He went after Conner. Did you keep Rachael in the car?" She carried the bulk of the weight of her grown son, had a husband who was chasing a madman through the wilderness, and still asked about her other child.

"Yes, with the doors locked. Will she know to stay that way?"

"She'd better." I don't know how long we walked but by the time we reached the bridge I was covered with Robert's blood and my legs gave out as soon as we loaded him into the car. Jillian checked the field dressing that Bill applied to Robert's waist and mumbled something about being grateful to be married to a doctor. Then she climbed into the front seat and started the car.

"Rachael, we will come back for Daddy but we have to get Robert to the hospital." Rachael just nodded. We were all numb and unsure of exactly what to do but Jillian was right, Robert needed emergency care. He groaned but didn't wake up. I held one hand on the bandage to keep steady pressure on the wound. All we could do was hope we got to the emergency room in time. Or was it already too late?

* * *

Bill saved his son's life by stopping the flow of blood, then he saved Miranda's life by chasing Conner away. Conner had more experience evading pursuers through the woods though, and Bill was running wild worried about his family. He didn't stand a chance of catching the man.

Conner reached his shelter in plenty of time to pack his bag and pull away at a leisurely pace. He hated that he didn't get rid of Miranda, but he knew it was time to leave Florida for good. After killing the boy tonight he knew that the search for him would become much more aggressive. If they found the bodies that he hid around the woods there would not be a safe place for him on the East Coast. Conner planned on getting as far as he could as fast as he could this time. He remembered Nina telling him that she traded lives with people from all over the world, so he was going to try California for a while or maybe New Mexico. Somewhere warm and near the border.

Chapter 44

I didn't slip for the rest of the day, and I don't think that anyone in Robert's family did either. We all sat in the waiting room, which was more like a long hall with chairs lined up on either side and waited to hear that Robert was going to live. Bill called Jillian from the woods and told her that Conner got away. Of course, he got away, I thought bitterly. The bad guy always got away. Who cared that he was a murderer? Who cared about the girls whose lives he took or tore apart? Not the local police, not karma, no one. I tried to shake my mindset and feel grateful because there was a part of me that was relieved that we were out of the woods metaphorically and literally, but somehow I could not shake my dissonance.

Robert recovered in the hospital over the next week. I slipped in and out of his room, in and out of my life, and somehow managed to keep up the last of my duties for graduation. Robert's teachers brought him his final assignments and made special arrangements so he could graduate on time. We played endless games of chess and discussed our plans for the coming year. Neither of us breached into asking the other if they wanted to try to see each other, to make room in our lives for whatever this was. Sometimes I thought it was because it was assumed that we would, and there was no need to ask. Other times I wondered and wanted to concrete us, but somehow that seemed trite. Some things don't need to be confirmed and a hospital room was not the place anyways.

My friends saw him in a new light. For whatever reason being shot gave him some type of mysterious edge. The fact he did it to save me from a kidnapper made him the talk of the town. I didn't care what they thought either way. I was just ready, so ready, to be done with them all. Ready to be a college student in another town where no one knew me well. I was accepted into UF, but I was thinking FSU was further and a better choice if they would have me. It was close enough that me and my parents could keep figuring out each other but far enough that I could maybe be me.

While I could muster up the desire to leave high school, my enthusiasm for the next phase was not coming. I was not sure what the source of my apathy was. After all, Kara and Rachael were fine. Robert was recovering physically, and mentally he was sharp as a tack. But everything felt blah. I discussed it with him during one of our late-night chats. He was the one to bring up depression, maybe he was right. Maybe the stress of the year and finally coming out about Maggie triggered something of a depression, but could you be depressed and still fall in love? I was drowning in the oddest combination of disinterest in so much about my life and complete fascination with a moody boy who had never let me down.

Graduation day arrived and I took my time applying my makeup exactly how I practiced and planned for four years. I had my hair blown out and then curled at the tips. I felt like this was the last time I would have to put on this mask. The last time I needed to be perfect. I didn't know what the future held at college but I knew that the image I upheld in high school would not be so meticulously maintained after this day. Maybe the past year of ups and downs gave me the courage to make that decision, or maybe it was Robert's never-care attitude that rubbed off on me. As I applied the dark brown M.A.C. shade of eye shadow I bought at the mall just for the occasion, I decided that after today anytime I got dolled up it would be strictly because I wanted to. I refused to wear my makeup and hair as a mask anymore. That was my graduation resolution. Was that a thing? Now it was.

We graduated on the football field with our parents in the stadium seats and the graduating class lined up before the podium. I listened to the keynote speaker, a local alumni and pro-baseball player talk about new beginnings and how fast the next few years would go by. All I could think about was how much I wanted to be gone. I forced myself to focus on his words and the words of the valedictorian who went next. I didn't let myself dwell on the fact that if all the drama of the past year didn't occur it would be me standing up there. I honestly didn't even care. I was just so ready to be gone. Then I was.

I slipped into a young child in daycare and suddenly I knew without a doubt that this was not a moment I wanted to be absent from.

"Dammit!" I shrieked and tossed my crayon across the room. A tired-looking woman came and sat next to me. She didn't seem surprised.

"What is going on today baby?" She picked up another color and placed it in my hand. I closed my eyes and tried as hard as I could to leave.

I thought about the hot sun, about how miserable I was underneath my graduation robe. I thought about my friends sitting on either side of me and of Robert three rows down.

Robert. That was it. I felt myself calm down and I was back in the hot sun baking under my green robe. As they called the names one by one I watched my classmates graduate and wondered where we would all end up. I no longer felt impatient at being there, but I did want to see Robert. They called his name while I was gone. When they called my name I beamed. I'm not even sure I walked up to the stage. I may have floated. After all, I earned this. Only I knew how lucky I was to be the one inside this moment. On my way back down I scanned the crowd and sat next to Robert for the rest of the ceremony.

"I slipped," I whispered once I was settled next to him.

"I slipped and I made myself return!" He turned to me as the meaning sunk in and a wide grin spread across his face. I leaned in as he did, and there in front of all my friends family and our whole graduation class, we kissed. The moment was perfect and it didn't slip away. The hope was tangible and the future was mine to grab. I could not put down the grin on my face and it was starting to hurt. I was still grinning like a fool as we threw our caps in the air and kissed once again. Maybe the fact that I controlled that one slip caused what happened next. Maybe it was something else altogether. All I know is if I could go back I would. I would go back to those moments and cherish every one of them.

Chapter 45

I woke up the next day in Rachael's cozy bedroom. The vanity against the wall and dim light through the curtains were becoming all too familiar. I don't know why she slipped into me again. She was not supposed to trade with anyone intentionally anymore. I got dressed and marveled at the newfound strength she had. Her cancer really was gone for good, it seemed.

"Good morning, Mrs. Matthews." I took Rachael's spot at the table. She studied Rachael's face for just a moment before she replied, "Miranda?"

"Yep."

"Well, good morning," she set a plate of eggs in front of me and asked me if I would call Rachael at my house. Before I could reply the phone rang.

"Hello. Hey baby, you don't need to be trading anymore with Miranda. We discussed this," she paused then added, "That's odd. Well, ask the Stones if you can come over please." She hung up the phone and turned to me, "she says she didn't trade on purpose." Jillian didn't seem too concerned so I decided not to worry about it either. After all, why would I? People slipped all the time. Robert staggered downstairs and rubbed the top of his sister's head before plopping down.

"Aw, come on!" I protested.

"Miranda is Rachael, and Rachael is on her way," Jillian informed him.

"Why the hell would she do that?" He searched my face.

"Watch your mouth. She said it was not intentional, she'll be here in a moment." Jillian told us to take care of the breakfast dishes and left the room. It took Rachael an hour and a half to make it fifteen minutes from my house.

"Sorry, your parents would not let me go. They are getting clingy over the idea of you leaving for college." She rushed to help Robert up the steps. He had not 100% recovered since he got shot. I could not help but notice how nice we looked together from the outside, and how weary Robert looked.

"When are you going to switch back with Miranda?"

"I have been trying all day. I don't know," Rachael sounded defensive. I still didn't worry about it. Why would I have?

It was not until the next day when I woke up in Rachael's body still that the first hint of worry broke through. When I slipped from her into a frazzled daycare worker, then back again, I knew that we had a real problem. I quickly went to search for Robert's Dad.

"Dr. Matthews?" He glanced up from his desk.

"Miranda?"

"Yes. I uh, we may have a problem," I went on to explain how I had slipped from Rachael to another person, then back to Rachael. He stood up and stared out the window.

"I think you need to get her over here and see if you can't get a hold of that atomic healer again." I felt bad at his tired expression but tried to remind myself that I had no choice in this predicament either. I tried the number Dr. Townsend left me over and over. I did an internet search only to discover he somehow disappeared. I even did a cachet page search, there was no mention of a Dr. Townsend in the Keys or any of the rest of the state. I thought about driving down there but with Rachael's body, I would not get too far. I hoped I would not be stuck at age fifteen for long. That night Rachael and I had a sleepover at my house. It was not for fun, it was so I could go home for a night. My mom was a mess bringing together the last of my graduation party and my grandparents were sleeping in the living room. I hated not being there as me, they didn't come over enough as is since they moved to Washington to escape the heat. I tried to hang out with them after dinner but Mom shooed us away and what could I do as Rachael?

I looked back and forth for Grammy to tell me it was okay and to sit down next to her as they poured over my old photo albums but Rachael had already gone to my room with my body and I was just stuck awkwardly. I sulked into my room and tried not to slam the door.

"I'm looking for something to go with your tan," Rachael said as she plundered through my nail polish box. She chose a peachy orange and began removing the teal I had just applied before the switch.

"Hey! I like that color."

"Don't blame me, blame your mom. She's on a kick about teaching you all the domestic chores you missed out on before you leave for college. I have baked enough for an army, then had to do the dishes to boot. I think she is going to miss you a lot, but doing the dishes ruined these nails." She applied the first layer of polish. She was right, it did look great with my summer tan. I felt my throat close up and tried to hide my jealousy. I wanted my body back. I wanted this time with my mom before I left for college.

"Whatever. Just put the polish back when you're done." I felt a little bad for snapping. It may not have been her fault, but she didn't have to enjoy being me quite so much.

The day of my graduation party started hot and bright. In Florida, May could be gentle but more days than not were hot, muggy, and brilliant. I loved it. I enjoyed the hottest months, but those transition times in May and September were my favorites. I never planned to attend my graduation party as a guest and watch someone else embrace my grandmother and smile brightly with my face at whatever it was she whispered in my ear. I won't lie, it was hard. Not being able to hold Robert's hand and seeing the way he chatted with Rachael while she inhabited my body was hard in a different way. There were a million things to worry about and a dozen to be upset about as I sat in the corner of my backyard at a rented table and listened to the people chatter around me. The one thing that was overtaking my mind, the one thought that was driving me down into the deepest depths was the fear that this was it. I would never be me again. I don't know how I knew it, but I knew it to the core of me.

Chapter 46

Rachael did have an it all started when moment. It all started when she switched places with Miranda for the last time. Sure, a million little things led up to that moment but it was a clear defining line for her. In the past two years, she battled cancer and helped save a kidnapping victim. She made new friends and grew from being a child to a shadow of the adult she would become. She even had her first kiss, albeit with Miranda's lips.

Things were complicated but there was one constant. The one thing she could always rely on as she fought for her life and fought for Kara to be saved was her family. Even when she felt she could not go on after chemotherapy sessions, her brother Robert shut in with her and tried his best to amuse her. He prayed with her and then cut her no slack. He was her best friend through it all. Then when Miranda came along like a breath of fresh air from a hot angry southern wind she had someone else she knew would always be in her corner.

Until she messed it all up by getting stuck. She literally stole Miranda's life and no matter how hard she tried she could not return it. It was the clear line between knowing no matter what happened she would be okay and she would have her family, and watching the people she loved start pulling away. They could deny it but it was true.

* * *

It hit Robert one evening, about two weeks after he came home and a few days after all the graduation events settled down, and it hit him like a ton of bricks. His family was sitting around after dinner watching television. Miranda was still Rachael and Rachael was visiting in Miranda's body. They had drifted into a routine, Rachael spent as much time as she could at her own home and Miranda spent as much time as she could with her parents but they did not really understand why Robert's kid sister seemed to tag along with their daughter so much. Everyone was waiting and it was wearing thin. Waiting for Miranda and Rachael to trade back and waiting for Robert to fully recover from his gunshot wounds. The wounds were mostly healed but the girls seemed to show no inclination of returning to themselves.

"This is it, isn't it?" he was not asking anyone in particular but he saw the look on Rachael's face. Miranda knew, she knew this was the way it was going to be. The look was a mixture of despair and worry for the family around her.

"What are you talking about Robert?" Rachael refused to meet his eyes.

"You and Miranda. We need to face it and start planning around the fact that this is how it is now. Whatever the hell it means to all of us." He looked around the room and decided he could not stand it. He had been cooped up too long. He let this problem go too long. He stood up and grabbed his truck keys, "Mom, I will be back later," he didn't look at his sister or his girlfriend in their various forms. He wanted to slam the door behind him, he wanted to yell at them both to stop doing this to him, but what was the point? He just left quietly, knowing that he was going to have to distance himself from the two most important people in his life for a while.

Driving the back roads was a blessing and a curse. He could smell Miranda's perfume on his seat, he could remember the taste of her and the way she felt against him the night they almost went too far. Any temptation to dwell on the memory was soured by the fact that his sister was not budging from Miranda. Who knew when she would?

He still loved her. He never even got to say the words to her face. He knew though, that if he did she would fight it and react in a way that he could not anticipate. Just like he knew that she would give him the same love back. The same love that was unlike anything he ever experienced. The kind that didn't need shallow affirmations, the kind that just was. It was the hand held even in anger. It was the look of lust even in mundane moments. Robert let himself get lost sometimes in the thoughts of what could have been. He imagined them both choosing the same college and going away together, steamy nights in dorm rooms, even breakups over trivial jealousy, and of course ending up together when it was all over. That someday was never going to come.

Miranda was gone as far as any romantic notion was involved. It was easy to say that, to know that as the truth, but it was impossible when looking into Rachael's eyes and feeling the same jolt that Miranda gave him when she was herself, or chatting with Rachael in Miranda's body and feeling sisterly towards her. He knew without a doubt that soul mates existed because his perspective of his sister and girlfriend shifted drastically. He knew the only thing to do was leave.

Chapter 47

The day I left for college was nothing like I planned it. After all, I planned to actually go. I didn't plan to stand in my parent's driveway watching my body drive away in the new blue Volvo that my Dad bought me for graduating. I stood there in my yard and bit back the tears. I felt like chasing the line of dust down the lime-rock road until she hit the brakes. She had to come back with my life. What was I supposed to do now?

Robert left without much show the week before. We talked long into the night but it was just one of those things that we could not work our way through. We could not fix this. I was stuck, for who knew how long, in his little sister's body. That didn't do much for the friendship, but it definitely put a complete halt to the romance. Rachael meanwhile, appeared to be enjoying the freedom of being me. After all, I just graduated, had a new car, and was about to enjoy living in a dorm at the University of Florida for the next year.

I envied her so bad it hurt, but mainly I just missed being me. I could not bring myself to hate her though. I could see the panic behind the smile. I could tell she was just trying her best to do what she could.

It wasn't until that moment when she pulled out of my drive

for good, and my parents both looked at me expectantly like they wondered why Rachael was still hanging out at their house now that Miranda had gone that it all really hit me.

I texted Mrs. Matthews to come to get me. The ride back home, or at least to Rachael's home, was mostly silent. We were all just doing what we could but with Robert gone and Rachael at college, I felt more than a little displaced.

Chapter 48

The first few weeks of college were a whirlwind and a relief for Rachael. She was trying to get used to calling herself Miranda full-time. It was not too difficult because she slipped into other lives for as long as she could remember. However, now and then she felt that if someone didn't call her her own name she would burst. On the other hand, it was great to be away from Miranda's parents who had her feeling guilty for not being who they thought and for stealing those moments from Miranda. It was also great to be away from her own family for similar reasons.

In her classes and her dorm room, no one had any expectations, no eager looks, the waiting game ended when she left that group of people. The weight that lifted was palpable. She may have still been someone else but at least no one knew it. The classes were not too hard, when they did get overwhelming she took advantage of the tutoring lab. Everything was set up for the success of a student willing to put in the effort, and Rachael was determined not to ruin Miranda's life any more than she already did. She could not bring herself to call her friend, but she could make sure she was holding the life she had been thrust into together until she returned it to her.

* * *

Conner spent the summer holed up in a weekly rental on the outskirts of Pasadena where no one looked twice at each other. He detested living at no-tell motels, but they had their perks. News of his spree had not reached the west coast and for the most part, he was able to move freely and search for his girls. His search brought no luck though.

No one smiled back at him with Grace's sweet charm, no one came close to Sophie's innocence, and he was sure if he was going to find Nina again it would have to be in Miranda Stone. That belief gave him the audacity to buy a used motorcycle and make his way back across the nation. He had a messy beard now and added a few tattoos. His farmer's tan was now a deep leather from hours riding the hills. Even his own girls would barely recognize him. He had no worries about the cops pulling him, his force was focused on a single social media post by Miranda's mother.

All it said was: *I could not be more proud of my daughter for choosing to go into Early Childhood Education, like me. What a legacy of love and service!* He scoffed at the not-so-humble brag but also knew to his core that Miranda's choice to become a teacher must be tied to the fact that his Nina was also an early education teacher. There was no way it was a coincidence. From the moment he read the post he knew his return was inevitable.

Chapter 49

Certain things helped a little. Perfectly applied eye shadow, and highlights that shaped my face to look fuller and my cheekbones higher, these little lies soothed the feeling. The feeling that came on sometimes when I was in a group of friends, came on for no apparent reason on the way to the bus stop or in the middle of a class. It was paralyzing and it stopped me in my tracks, but I could not stop. I had to show up to school, I had to smile at my friends, and I had to keep face no matter how many I wore. So I would try to fight it off but it hurt. I felt naked and so raw that it literally hurt as if my cheekbones were exposed and anyone who spoke to me could see the rot of the bones beneath the flesh but they were too polite to say that I made them sick and that they had to get away as fast as possible. I would try to fight past the instinct to hide away, and it would work, most of the time.

I considered it a success if I didn't go home sick, or worse, hide out in a bathroom stall until the crowds passed. I didn't overcome anything though. I just secured the mask a little tighter. I made sure to hide myself a little deeper. Those days I would be a little louder and a little faster with the punch lines. If they were distracted by labeling me as the dumb one, or the funny one, then they would not see me. That was the last thing

I wanted, to be seen. On those days slipping was the best thing that could happen. I didn't feel like a raw nerve when I was hiding away from me. Being Rachel and doing high school over again was not a bit easier, it was ten times harder.

Sometimes fear would weigh so heavy that I would retreat inside. So deep inside that when someone spoke to me I would have to swim to the surface to reply. These days were the worst, the exposed nerves were unable to be covered by any persona and I wanted to hide away forever. These days didn't come often as long as I stayed on top of my game, as long as I cultivated the image everyone expected to see. I thought those days were behind me. I already graduated high school there was no reason for me to be in tenth grade again doing this all over, but here I was, reliving the years I was so happy to see gone.

I couldn't even bring myself to do it differently this time. I put on the same armor and followed the same routine as I did the first four years I went through high school. Except this time I was Rachael, the dark-haired cancer survivor who was known for her brain. When I was me, I could embrace the ditsy side but it didn't come off so easy in Rachael's body. Everyone watched her a little closer. She was already known as being the smart one, and even though the cancer was cleared, the cheer moves I could once do easily didn't come as smoothly in her body. I don't know if I just didn't have the heart for it anymore or if it was her, but either way, she/I did not make the team when we tried out. I should have been relieved that the pressure to perform would not be there, but I truly looked forward to the escape of the movement and the anonymity of being a part of the group.

Each week ticked on and I did my best to keep her grades perfect and her friends happy. Her parents spent many weekends in Gainesville. I started staying home when they left. Somehow I felt like I was intruding when I tagged along with them for the visits to their daughter in my life.

* * *

Robert drove north when he left his parent's house. He got a job with a landscaping company in Brunswick, Georgia. Then he moved on to scrape barnacles off of the bottom of boats in a marina in Charleston. He worked part-time, turned in the bare minimum in his online classes, and tried not to think of the people he left at home at all.

Robert ran because being home with Miranda as Rachael tore him up, and not being near Rachael as Miranda was just as painful. It all hurt too much and although it felt like a choice, in hindsight, he saw that he reacted like a dog in a trap. He reacted without thought or plan to the pain that overtook him. After a few months, he realized his mistake but he didn't know if it was too late. The first step was a visit home, then he would find Rachael because that is what he should have done from the start.

* * *

There was a moment each day when the pain was bearable, a fleeting moment when the panic threatening to boil over calmed down enough to breathe. It was that last moment of sleep, the eternity in between Elysium and the real world. It lasted only a few minutes and it lasted a lifetime. Long enough to keep Rachael sane but never long enough to allow her any joy to carry away when the last strands of nod faded. Long enough to allow her to forget that she was stuck in someone else's life, long enough to be herself for a moment. When she slept she dreamed many of the same types of dreams she always did regardless of who she was in at the time, but in that moment right before she was awake it was almost like being normal again. Almost.

She lay in her twin bed and traced the pattern of the concrete block underneath thick layers of glossy white paint. She knew she had a class in an hour and should get up and start to get dressed and review her notes, but she could not seem to bring herself to do it. She could list in her mind all the reasons she should have already been out the door as the minutes ticked by but she still could not leave the safety of her cocoon. By the time she got out of bed, it was too late to get dressed so she just slipped on a pair of flip-flops and pulled her hair into a messy bun. Miranda would have never let herself be seen this way, but Rachael didn't let herself dwell on what Miranda would do. It was hard enough to be Miranda without thinking about her all the time. Besides no one noticed her these days anyways.

* * *

When I got off the bus I saw Robert's car in the driveway and I had to resist the urge to run inside to greet him. After all, he was probably home despite me, not to see me. I quickly hung my sweater on the hook and tried to retreat to Rachael's room before anyone noticed me.

"Miranda." Just hearing his voice saying my name made my face flush and tears well up behind my eyes. I hated myself at that moment and I wanted to run and hide.

"I should not have run away." Robert pulled me tight and although his sister's body was shorter than mine and I could not get lost in the moment too much it still felt like coming home. I had not felt such peace in months. I melted into him. After a moment, he pulled away and we went into his mother's tidy kitchen. He poured a glass of milk and tossed a Little Debbie snack cake at me. I set the cookie on the counter.

"So how was school?" He didn't meet my eyes. I had a head full of snarky comments but I didn't say a word. I couldn't find the ones that cut deep enough, the ones that hurt him as bad as I hurt, and the ones that did float up left me too exposed. They would show him how badly I needed him, how much he could hurt me. I knew my words would not make him stay when he was ready to move on. They could not fix anything.

I did not have to say anything though.

"Miranda, I made a mistake and I'm so sorry. Things got hard. I didn't even know how wrong it was for me to go until seeing you just now. All I can say is I'm sorry."

"I missed you," it hurt to say the words but I needed him to see me and to know it.

He hung out with his family for the evening and the next day after school he picked me up.

"We need to go see Rachael. Mom said you stopped going with them, that it got too hard. I think it's time, Miranda." I didn't argue. I didn't mind seeing her, even if she was in me. In fact, I missed my friend. It just all felt so weird lately.

Maybe I was guilty of my own form of running from the situation. We drove straight to Gainesville. I knew right where Rachael's dorm room was because I helped her decorate every inch of it. We decided to wait in the lobby near the entrance for her to return from her afternoon class. The last I heard she took a full course load and was doing amazing. I hoped I was keeping up my end of things as well as she seemed to be according to her and my mom's social media. We did not have to wait too long before she walked by us.

I almost did not recognize myself. She looked like any other student around here in a pair of yoga pants, flip-flops, and a messy bun but I was almost speechless at the sight of me so casual in the middle of the day. Maybe it was because I was technically not a student, so I was not as relaxed here as her, but I had to bite my tongue to resist asking her when she last had her toes done and where she got that garish orange football shirt. She looked incredibly tired, I wondered if she was getting any sleep while earning me all those great grades. As soon as she saw us she dropped her bag and leaped into her brother's arm. They hugged for a moment.

Then she turned to me, "Oh wow it is amazing to see y'all both." She ushered us into her dorm room and I was surprised to find it exactly how I left it when we decorated it a few months ago. I would have assumed that she would have personalized it by now.

"Are y'all hungry? I slept in and did not get a chance to eat all day. We could go to dinner? As a family?" She was such an odd combination of child and woman. I suddenly felt like crap for avoiding her because I was jealous. She may look just like an eighteen year old ready to take on college but she was only fifteen and had never been away from her family. I wondered if her parent's weekly visits were enough. Somehow I doubted she made a circle of friends to replace them, and me and Robert abandoned her months ago. I pulled her close and gave her the same apology that Robert gave me the day before. I hoped she accepted it.

"Rachael, Miranda is right. We are both so sorry. This whole thing is a mess but the biggest mistake we could make is to separate and shut each other out. Let's go get dinner, and you can decide if you forgive us." Robert headed towards the door.

"I don't have to forgive y'all. I just hope you can forgive me if this ends up being a permanent thing. I don't ever dare say it in front of Mom and Dad, but I'm slipping like normal, and returning to Miranda's body as if it's home every time."

"Let's just all agree that this sucks but it's no one's fault. I hate to tell you this, but slipping is the same for me too. In and out I go, randomly, but I always return right here like it's home. I patted my heart."

Robert opened the door and we both followed him out. It seemed that nothing else needed to be said about who was sorry and when this would be over. Dinner was perfect, I don't even remember where we ate or what I ordered, only that it was crowded and we all made small talk about school and grades and silly things. I felt normal for the first time in months. I reached out at one point and held Robert's hand, just for a moment. His eyes went soft at my touch and his smile was real. The moment was broken by Rachael.

"Please don't kiss, guys. That would be too weird." She tossed her straw paper at her brother to lighten her words but the moment was long gone.

"I would never." Robert looked ashamed. I felt it. He might never because he looked at me and saw her. I don't know that I could say the same thing, no matter what form I was in. The spell on the evening was not broken and when we left for dinner Rachael gave us a tour of the campus. It was beautiful and I looked forward to joining her in two years, if I was not myself by then. When we parted that evening we vowed to come back as often as we could, if she would start coming home to sleep over on the weekends.

As we pulled away in Robert's truck I already missed her and asked Robert to do a loop around the neighborhood when we saw the red light on outside of Krispy Kreme. We could use fresh donuts as an excuse to drop back in, just for a moment. I ran in and got a hot dozen for her and another batch for the road and we were back at her dorm in less than ten minutes.

It is amazing what can happen in ten minutes. When we reached her dorm the door was left ajar. The neat area we left was destroyed. The calendar was torn from the wall and her comforter was on the floor. It looked like someone struggled, but we could not find a hint of her aside from the mess. I rushed out into the empty hall and beat on the door across from hers. No one answered. The hall was empty this time of day. What happened? I went down the row beating on every door until finally I found a room that was occupied.

"What in the world are you carrying on for?" The girl who opened the door did not look much older than I was. She had a golden face mask and a robe on and looked deeply annoyed.

"My sister is missing and her room is torn up, she's right down there," I pointed at her open door, "have you heard anything?"

She softened a bit, "go to the last door on the left. The RA keeps video surveillance of the hall at all times and she is usually home unless she has a class. She is a TA too."

I did not try to decipher her words, I just ran down to the last door and started beating on it. Robert caught up with me just as she opened it. As soon as we explained the situation she pulled out her phone and pushed a few buttons. When she showed us the screen my entire world closed in.

Immediately after we left Rachael returned to her room and a man in motorcycle leathers and a thick beard knocked on the door. She swung it wide open like she was expecting a friend and he rushed in instantly. A few moments later he walked out with her in his arms without a care in the world. It appeared that he was relying on luck to get her out of the building and his luck held. No one else entered the hall until we did five minutes later. I fell to the floor as Robert dialed 911. There was no way this could be happening, not again.

The Resident Advisor made some calls and then informed us that the security footage from the parking lot and outside the building would be sent to her by the time the deputies arrived. All we would do was wait for the footage and the campus police.

The footage came first. The second it loaded I recognized the face that looked full-on into the camera. The beard could not hide those haunted eyes. Conner Adams was back. The Man had Rachael

Chapter 50

Robert sank to the floor once he realized there was not anything he could do for his sister. He sat there with his head folded into his knees until his parents arrived. He just felt numb and useless. A part of him wanted to get in his truck and head to I-75 to chase down the white rental car that the security footage showed Conner drive away in but there was no telling which direction he went or if the man even went to the interstate.

His parent's arrived in record time, and Miranda's parents were close behind. They did not explain their presence at Miranda's kidnapping scene. After all, what could they say? "It's actually my daughter in Miranda's body?" No one questioned them anyways. The area soon became crowded with crime scene techs, detectives, and loitering students. No one could believe the notorious serial killer could just walk into the dorm room and carry out his victim in the middle of the day.

Robert knew exactly how he did it. Conner Adams had time to learn his sister's habits and found a weakness at the right time of day. Robert hated the acute awareness he had of the fact that Conner would not have been able to get close enough to observe schedules if Rachael was not so alone here on campus. If he visited more often, then his sister and Miranda's body would be safe and the whole family would not be reliving this garish nightmare. He sat silently in his self-contempt until his phone buzzed. He answered it and didn't recognize the voice but he knew instantly it was his little sister.

"Robert, I don't know how long I have. It's Conner. He took me, I think he drugged me, and I think we are going north on the interstate based on a few signs I see from the floorboard. He's in a little car and he has a beard now. I don't know much else."

"Rachael, I'm so sorry we are going to get you out of this I promise."

"I wish I could think of more to say."

"Don't worry. Just keep him happy and get yourself away as soon as you can. Call every time you slip," Robert's voice cracked and his mom grabbed the phone.

Robert listened as she told her daughter that she loved her and they would find her. Jillian was crying but trying to hide it from Rachael. After a bit, her tone changed and Robert knew that his sister was back with the monster. Jillian got information from the person who slipped into the situation but she did not have anything else to add. After that, they texted an anonymous tip to the deputies that Conner was headed north and they all got in their vehicles and decided to head in that direction themselves. They did not let Miranda's parents know they were leaving. It was hard enough to explain why Jillian was as upset as Miranda's own mother. It was another surreal and inexplicable situation that the Matthews had unfortunately become accustomed to.

* * *

I hated leaving my parents. They looked hollowed out and I just wanted to hug them both and say it was going to all be okay. I was Rachael though, and there was nothing I could do for them except help get their daughter's body back, even if I would not be the one in it.

I felt horrible for what Rachael may be going through, and I knew that Robert was about to lose control of the fear. It was in all his body language, from the stiff way he opened the door for me, to the way he gripped his steering wheel like it would make his truck beacon to his sister's location. We drove silently on the interstate for a while, just above the speed limit but not enough to get the attention of the deputies who were also searching the roads. I studied every vehicle, not just the white sedans. Who knows if Conner changed at some point?

I slipped at some point into a cheerleader, of all things. I would have loved the chance to relive my old life, except my heart was completely frozen and I could not even pull myself together enough to pretend. I told the other girls I had a migraine and left the group to hide in the dark until I slipped back. It only took about an hour. Robert and his parents were standing in a gas station parking lot filling up their tanks when I returned.

"Any new information?" I asked.

"No, Miranda, I'm sorry. We are filling up and headed to his camp at Rocky Creek. It's a lark considering that he'd have to be a fool to return there, but he was audacious enough to pull her right from her room," Robert's dad explained but seemed a bit disconnected. I guess when you don't have any good choices you make the best one you can then question yourself the whole time.

I didn't reply. He didn't need me to. We were all wound tight and about to snap. We got back on the road and headed north. When Robert's cell rang he answered almost instantly, he did not take his eyes off the road but I could tell it was Rachael.

"What do you mean off? Of course, he's off he lost his mind years ago."

"Oh. OH." He handed me the phone and slammed on the gas to overcome his parents. I held on to the phone and my seat belt as he careened towards their car.

"This is Miranda, Rachael what is going on? Robert is driving like a maniac."

"I told him that Conner took me to a motel. It's right off the interstate near the Georgia line, at least I think so because the advertisements are for pecans and oranges. It looks deserted but I guess it's open cause he checked us in. He's acting even weirder than he used to, Miranda. I don't know what he has planned, he gave me another shot in the leg of something that makes me not be able to move but I can hear and see. It's really bad, Miranda." She started to cry and I started to cry but I tried to hide it from Robert. I did not know what to say to her but I knew I had to be strong. She was the one in the situation, even if I would trade her in a heartbeat if I could.

"Okay, baby. Here's what I think you should do. I may be wrong but I don't think I am. Act like his daughter. Make sure he does not think you're Nina. You have to be one of the little girls. The last time he took me he thought I was Nina, that may be why he was obsessed with getting my body again." I got chills at the implication, and I know she understood when her sobs became rougher.

"His daughters' names are Grace and Sophie. Choose one and do your best to make him believe that you are not Nina or me. Rachael, you can do this. I know you can."

Robert got his parents to pull over and I handed Jillian the phone again as they plotted which motel she might be at. Once I no longer had Rachael to be strong for I went behind Robert's truck and vomited all over the grass. No one paid me any mind. We all loaded back up in the vehicles and headed to the exit that they decided was most likely to have a no-tell motel and both Georgia and Florida tourist information. It did not narrow it down terribly but it was more to go on than before.

"That was good advice you gave her, to act like his daughters, not his wife. Do you think she can pull it off?" Robert was grasping at the same straws I was.

"I think she has to," I answered honestly. I didn't even have it in me to sugarcoat. He reached out and held my hand for a while. I closed my eyes, laid my head back against the headrest, and tried to think of anything else I could come up with to help Rachael if she slipped and called again.

Chapter 51

Rachael was stuck in the nightmare again. She was in an aquarium swimming from end to end over and over with no progression. Robert would tap on the glass and she would go to his finger to try to interact. Then the rest of her family would join in staring and tapping and peering through the water glass and air that separated them. They were talking and then yelling and the tapping increased. She swam behind the garish fake coral reef and stared as they continued to tap louder and louder until the glass started to crack and the water seeped out.

Rachael woke up gasping for air. She looked around discreetly hoping Conner did not notice her. She could not hide her shock when she saw her brother sitting next to her in the driver's seat of his pick-up.

"Robert! Am I me?" she cried out.

"Miranda?"

"No. No, it's me, Rachael, it's really me!" Robert had to pull over on the side of the road. After he stopped the car he got out and hugged his sister.

"I can't believe you were finally able to switch back." He held her close then they both hurried back to his truck. The urgency to get Miranda's body back was not lessened now that Rachael was not the one in it. Robert handed Rachael his phone to call their parents. Rachael stayed on the phone until they got off on the last exit before Georgia. Rachael quickly dismissed the area and Robert backtracked an exit while Rachael and his parents drove forward into exit one in Georgia.

As soon as Robert pulled off the freeway and saw PECANS, ORANGES, and BABY GATORS in worn lettering over a fruit stand he knew he was at the right place. He took a picture of the sign and sent it to the group chat but did not wait for Rachael to confirm before he continued looking for the dingy motel she described. It did not take long. As soon as he saw the faded blue paint he got chills down his spine. He only hoped he was not too late.

* * *

I was back in my body but I could not celebrate in all the ways I imagined I would over the past several months. In fact, I had to pretend, still, that I was not myself. I was practically a pro at this point anyways. Conner had my wrists handcuffed to the bedposts but my legs were free. I don't think the handcuffs even mattered much because I could not lift a finger. Whatever he was stabbing into my leg must have been a powerful concoction. I wondered how much more I could take before I had an overdose.

He stepped out of a doorway, I wondered how long he was standing there watching. When he saw me watching him he grinned and went to a black bag sitting on a worn dresser.

"I need you to sleep just a while longer, baby doll. I've got some business to tend to but I will be right back." The man who walked towards me looked a lot like the Conner who

197

kidnapped me before, but he was different in so many ways. More unhinged, for sure. He smelled terrible and his skin was tanned so much he was almost unrecognizable. He would fit more into a biker bar than the cop's uniform from his previous life. Nearly as soon as I felt the hot pinch of the needle in my thigh the whole world went dark.

* * *

Robert parked right behind the small white sedan and instantly charged the motel door directly in front of the parking spot. Busting a door in was not as easy as it looked in the movies. He threw his weight into it time and time again until he realized it was futile then he started rapping on all the windows down the lane as he made his way to the front desk. He didn't have a plan and it didn't cross his mind that he might be putting Miranda at greater risk. He was in full panic mode and would question every moment of it in retrospection.

When he got to the front office he found the door boarded with plywood. He slowly made his way back to the sedan as he pieced things together in his mind. When he reached the car he saw instantly what he was blind to in his rush to get to Miranda. The white sedan was the only vehicle in the lot. He walked back to the door that he was trying to tear down and turned the handle. He was too numb to feel surprised when the handle gave. He went into the room and found it empty. No bed, nothing in the room, not even carpet. He called his parents.

"She's not here. I think he set us up, but I don't even know how he would know to do it." His parents still came to the motel to see if Rachael saw anything familiar. She confirmed that she was awake when they pulled into the lot but he knocked her out again right after. She assumed it was so he could move her into the room, now they wondered if it was so she would not know she was moved into a new vehicle. They called and reported the white sedan to the police on Miranda's case, anomalously, of course. Then they all went to a local diner to recharge and figure out what to do next.

Although they were all happy to have Rachael back dinner was quiet and the waitress probably thought they were coming from a funeral. It certainly felt like it. Robert could not even remember what he ordered. The cell phones were all lined up on the table in case Miranda tried to call. Each moment that ticked by that they did not hear from her the tension at the table rose.

"I hope you all go about this with the same energy, even though it is not me with Conner anymore," Rachael did not have to say it though. The relief to have her back did not slow down their search or urgency. It simplified things to have the girls in their correct bodies, but it did not solve the problem in any real way. After dinner, they stood in the parking lot, at a loss for their next step.

"We could continue to the hunting camp like we originally planned. It's something at least," Robert argued.

"The last time we were there you got shot, and Conner had the upper hand the whole time. Let's get some evidence he's stupid enough to return where he knows the FBI is watching before we just trek out into the wilderness," Jillian argued.

She was right and Robert knew it, but going home did not feel right either. They decided to continue north, at least a few exits into Georgia just to see if they had any clearer ideas of what to do while they waited for any type of news

Chapter 52

onner had every aspect thought out. No one notices the homeless. As long as they stay on the sidelines and do not intrude they are practically invisible to most people. He never dared to step off the sidewalk onto the campus. The only time he braved Miranda's dorm was when he was in a janitor's uniform and he changed a bulb in the hall. He left before anyone batted an eye. He knew that people like his wife and daughters had an upper hand and he was not going to let Miranda use her ability to fly out of her body to her benefit. The right cocktail of drugs kept her asleep and groggy enough to manipulate easily. He made sure she saw the signs and the motel that was easy to describe. He hoped that his clues kept anyone searching long enough for him to get settled in with his wife and allow her to wear off the sedatives and return to him for real.

The cabin he took her to was not his. He found it when he was on the run. It was empty then and each time he checked on it he found it completely undisturbed. It was not uncommon for hunters to leave their holdings empty on lease land for most of the year. He already checked the property thoroughly for signs of game cams, beaten trails, or any human evidence. It seemed that this place had not been used, even seasonally, in a long time. It was located on the outskirts of the Okefenokee National Forest. The area was all but forgotten by everyone but the old-timers that lived in the tiny town on the edge of the swamp. He was confident he could live comfortably there with his wife until they both passed on, whenever that may be. At this point, he did not care when he ended as long as it happened with Nina by his side.

* * *

When I woke again the sun seemed to be coming up, but it could have been going down. I had little concept of time. Conner was sleeping next to me on the bed snoring loudly. I strained against the cuffs. If I got loose I don't know if I would have ran or tried to strangle him with my bare hands, come what may. My movement woke him and he turned to me in curiosity.

"Daddy?"

"That ain't going to work Miranda," he was smug. I never hated someone so much in my life.

"I don't know what you mean, Daddy. Please give me breakfast. Maybe pancakes and apples again. I'm hungry." I didn't have to fake the tears, I was scared out of my mind, but they didn't work anyway. He stood and went into the bathroom. I heard the shower start and listened as he took his sweet time. He was completely unconcerned about a thing. His manic surety frightened me more than anything else. When he got out of the shower he wore only a towel. I refused to look at him. When he crossed the room and removed the cuffs from both my hands I still kept my eyes on the green patchwork quilt.

It was not until he left the room and me unrestrained that I dared to look around and stand up. The room was small with a bed and a dresser. There was a door leading to the bathroom and a door leading to the rest of the home. I slowly turned the handle and was shocked to find it unlocked. When I stepped into the small living room I found Conner sitting on the worn wood-framed couch as if we were family. Whatever he was doing felt like warfare, but I could not put my finger on why. It was okay, two could play psychological games. If he took me to the woods to pretend I was Nina and have a second honeymoon, I would make sure he only saw his daughters in my eyes. I did not have to convince him entirely, just enough to make him doubt.

"Daddy, my tummy hurts." I didn't use a baby voice or exaggerate my movements. I tried to talk like I was a bored seven-year-old with a tummy ache.

"The bathroom is right there, this place is not that big. Do I need to show you where Miranda?" He picked up a dusty catalog of hunting gear and guns and stared intently at the pages.

"Stop calling me that. I'm Sophie." I stomped out of the room and into the bathroom. There was nothing in sight that I could use for a weapon, except maybe the toilet plunger but I did not feel strong enough to do much damage with it. I quickly finished up and headed back to the living room. He was still reading his paper. I went to ask for breakfast again but before I could get the words out I slipped into a high school classroom. I instantly jumped up out of the desk and ran from the room with the person's book bag. As soon as I got in the privacy of a bathroom stall I pulled out her phone and used the thumbprint to unlock it. Most sliders used thumbprint lock screens, but occasionally you would find one that preferred more privacy. I could not imagine what I would do if that was the case this time. Robert answered on the first ring.

"Miranda?"

"Yes! It's me."

"Where are you?"

"He's got me in a cabin. I've never seen it before. I have not been outside and he had me drugged the whole ride there. I don't know much."

"Anything Miranda, any little thing may help," Robert's voice cracked and I wondered if he had been to sleep since I left.

"I don't know anything. He untied me and is casual about my freedom. I don't know why that is. Maybe we're very remote or maybe he's just crazy. I have only been awake about half an hour."

"I'm so sorry about this," Robert sounded pained.

"This has nothing to do with you and I'm happy to get my body back. It's been a while you know." I tried to joke to lighten the mood but neither of us laughed. The bell rang and the bathroom flooded with girls talking, so I told Robert I would call him back if I had any information. I didn't know what else to do. He said he would call this number later to talk about what the girl who traded with me saw. It was a plan. It made us both feel a little in control. It was something.

* * *

Conner knew that Miranda would slip eventually and he did not want her tied up when she did. When his Nina came back to him he wanted her happy to see him, not yelling at him about kidnapping like last time. The cabin was remote enough that he had little worries about her getting away without him being able to track her relatively quickly, but the front door was jammed from the outside just to buy him a little time if she tried. It was easy enough to climb in the window after pushing the chair against the handle. Now it was a waiting game. He noticed when she slipped now, for the most part. This new person was polite, but not conniving.

She was not Miranda but definitely not Nina either. Conner gave her a plate of eggs and toast and she picked at it, uninterested at first. Then he heard her stomach growl and the girl laughed and asked when they ate last.

"Sorry sweetie, we got in too late for dinner." The girl did not appear to notice his leer. She dug into the eggs and then sat on the couch to flip through one of the magazines that littered the coffee table.

"Aw, my mom has the same bear in her bathroom." She pointed to the kitschy toilet paper holder that looked like a bear handing the roll, "I always wondered where she found it," the girl flipped to the front of the catalog and noticed the mailing address. Maybe that would give her a clue about her name since the man had not addressed her yet. There was an address label that said Smith, and Fargo, GA. Hmm. The girl snickered. She was from Fargo, North Dakota, what a fun coincidence. It was snowing there. She glanced out the window and saw bright sunshine and a large pine blocking the view.

"Let's go for a walk, I would love to feel some of that sunshine." The man glanced at her leggings and t-shirt before he answered, "No, too cold." There was something in his tone that kept her from arguing, but she did walk over to the window and study the green palmettos.

Whatever was going on here did not give her the best vibes, but it was still more interesting than the Algebra and English Lit classes she was missing. The slip only lasted about an hour and a half and the girl forgot it almost instantly when she returned to herself. She heard her phone ringing in the hall between classes and quickly put it on vibrate. She did not notice that she had nearly twenty missed calls from the same number until her mom picked her up after school. She finally answered once she was settled in the car.

The voice on the other end of the line instantly started talking without an introduction. "You slipped into my friend this morning. She is in a lot of trouble with a really bad guy, can you tell me anything, anything at all that might give us a way to help her?"

"Yes. Yes, I think I can. I knew that place gave me a bad vibe!" She tapped her mom on the arm and put the phone on speaker. "So your friend was not there by choice?" she asked so her mom would be up to date.

"No, she was taken yesterday from her college dorm you may have seen the story on the news?" Robert was getting a little impatient.

"No, I don't watch the news."

"Maria, do you have any information for this guy?" her mother prodded.

"Yes, I do. I was bored so I picked up a dusty old magazine on the table and I noticed it said Fargo, GA. I only remember because I am from Fargo, North Dakota. Also, the name on the address was Smith but there was no first name so I did not know what to call the guy."

"Wow. Thank you. Is there anything else?" Robert was excited about the information but also ready to get off the phone and use it.

"Not really. He would not let me go for a walk, but I was not tied up or anything. I ate eggs and he just kind of pretended to be busy while he watched me."

"Call this number if you remember anything, you may have saved her life." Robert hung up the phone and called the tip into the detective on Miranda's case. All these anonymous tips were going to lead back to him but he could not keep information away that might help save her. He took the information to his parents and they all celebrated the lucky find, then quickly realized it only narrowed down her location slightly. Fargo might be a little town, but there were miles of forest and swamp around it. The last name Smith was a lead, assuming the person who got the mail also owned the property. A quick search of the county property appraisal website showed a tract of land that consisted of nearly 2000 acres belonging to three different people with the last name Smith. Apparently, it was family land. None of it had a current home listed, but Bill explained that if the home were built before electric lines, or only used for non-residential purposes like a hunting camp then it may still show as just land, so all hope was not lost. 2000 acres was a pretty big tract to search, but it was a whole lot more to go on than they had at the beginning of the day. Once again, Robert sent the information to the detectives via the anonymous tip hot line. He wondered how many of the crime tips came from people who slid into other lives and could not explain where they got the information.

They did not hesitate once they had a general address. There was a moment of deliberation about bringing Rachael but she won the argument when they all realized they were wasting time trying to get her to stay. The Google directions said it would be an hour to get to Fargo. Robert hoped that they would not be too late. There were endless ways Conner could hurt Miranda and each and every one of them played in Robert's mind as he drove the empty roads to the swampland.

Chapter 53

I was actually bored. Who knew being abducted by a madman waiting for his dead wife to show up in your eyes could become mundane? We stayed in that small cabin until just before dark. He kept studying me waiting for me to slip, but it never happened and he never believed me when I pretended to be his daughter.

As the sun began to set he gave up his wait and asked me to join him on a walk around the property to check on things. I didn't have a choice so I agreed, but I did want to go. I knew better than to make a run for it without a plan but I could start scouting out the area for opportunity. He sent me to the room while he opened the door. I'm not sure exactly what he did, but I think I heard a window slide open and shut again. When he came to get me the front door was wide open. He held out his hand for mine as if we had the cozy habit of walking property at dusk together daily.

The walk went by way too fast because it got dark. There was nothing else on the property anyways. The small cabin looked historic from the outside with unpainted rough board siding and porches on the front and back. There was nothing particularly interesting that I could find to report back if I slipped again, except maybe the fact that the plants looked local so we did not go too far, but too far was relative and did not narrow down my location in any real way.

When we returned to the cabin I was sent to the bathroom while he locked the door to his satisfaction. When I came out he was chopping potatoes into cubes. I tried not to look at the knife, but it was there between us like an emblem of hope and fear. I played out scenarios in my mind. If I tried to get the knife from him I knew he would not give it up and I would likely end up injured. I doubted I could sneak it. I settled into the chair and tried not to show my disappointment. The knife may as well not exist. I was just too weak compared to him. He hummed as he opened a can of ham. My stomach growled despite itself. He grinned when he heard it.

"Miranda, we are going to be here together until Nina comes around. We may as well be friends. Come on, you can score the ham while I heat some brown sugar to make a glaze. It's not much but it actually turns out great for canned dinner. Nina loved it when we camped."

He handed me a butter knife and told me to cut diamonds onto the outer edges of the ham so his sugar-spice mixture could take hold. I didn't even consider using it as a weapon. I started scoring the pink meat like I would if I was in the kitchen with my dad.

"How long have you owned this place?" I tried to make small talk and maybe get a clue or two.

He just chuckled and did not answer for a moment. "I don't own it. I guess it is a hunting lease, we got lucky they keep the power on and the propane stocked. A fridge would have been nice." He handed me a Coke from the cooler with a proud smile, "We make do though, don't we honey?"

I popped the top then continued to question him, "So when

Nina shows up what's your big plan?"

"I guess I will hug my wife and tell her I missed her. Then we can plan how to get our daughters together."

I didn't try to explain to him how delusional he was. "If she comes will you let me go?"

"I'll do whatever she tells me to. She's in this world, she knows how it works. None of y'all have been any help. Seems like a dad trying to find his girls would appeal to your heart, but not a single one of you has ever helped me."

I didn't ask how many of us he captured. I didn't want to know. I did file away the fact that if he believed I was Nina he would be more pliable. I had no idea how I would pull it off though.

"Nina, Sophie, and Grace were so happy with me. I promise. I tried every day to be the dad my girls deserved and the best husband I could be. It's not fair. I'm going to get my chance to do it again." He tossed the potatoes into the cast iron pan with a little too much force and some fell to the floor.

I noticed his brown sugar and spice mixture was starting to boil up in the saucepan. I didn't have time to plan what happened next, everything went on pure reaction. I grabbed the bubbling syrup pot and poured it directly on the top of his head as he leaned to grab the fallen potatoes. He yelped in pain and fortuitously turned his head upwards to defend himself. The remainder of the molten sugar went directly onto his eyes and face. At this point he was a raging monster but lucky for me he was entirely blinded. I ran to the opposite corner of the room as he felt around him for me. His hand connected to the knife and he started waving it in front of him. I would have laughed at the garish sight but I knew if he honed in on me he would not hesitate to charge. I did not move, I did not breathe, and I barely dared to think. I suddenly realized I could slip and everything would be lost. The fear almost made me cry out but I stood against the wall and prayed with everything that I had that I would survive this moment.

He took a few steps and then collapsed to his knees. The knife fell to the floor between us. I still did not move. He fainted forward onto the floorboards. The house filled with smoke from the potato pan and the smell of burnt flesh and sugar was equally appalling, but I still did not move.

When the smoke overtook the room I started coughing and snapped out of myself. I reached forward and grabbed the knife. Then I stood above Conner for a moment debating whether I had the physical ability to drive the blade into his back. I didn't wonder if I could mentally handle it. I wanted to do it. I wanted to know that he could never get a hold of me or Rachael, or Kara, or any other little girl again. I started coughing just as I lifted the knife to bring it down into him. As I tried to catch my breath I noticed blue lights glaring through the curtain-less window. I rushed to the door but it was still blocked from the outside. Luckily, the first window I tried lifted easily and I stepped over the sill. I tumbled down the steps unable to catch my breath and I fell into the cool grass. Then everything went black.

Chapter 54

The image of Miranda staggering out of the window of the old cabin and charging down the steps with a butcher knife before collapsing in the yard was not one any of the Matthews would soon forget.

Robert thought she looked like a death goddess. Her hair, a wild halo, and a ferocity in her expression that was nothing short of otherworldly. Rachael thought she looked scared out of her mind and knew the feeling from being in her shoes. Both Jillian and Bill felt so much relief at seeing her alive that they did not pay mind to her appearance even as they all discussed the events later on.

Her parents arrived shortly after the detectives and ambulances. They rushed to her side and her mother insisted on riding in the ambulance with Miranda. It was a long slow cavalcade out of the swamp that night and the locals could not believe a notorious serial killer would hole up in their neck of the woods.

The cabin did not burn down and the owner put it up as a Haunted Air BnB as soon as the FBI cleared out the body and released the scene.

Conner's death was officially ruled as a heart attack. His melted face did not make the headlines, but Robert stayed to see him zipped into the body bag and knew without a doubt that the man did not die from the heart attack alone.

Miranda recovered in the hospital overnight, but she was surprisingly unscathed, physically. When she returned to her house the next afternoon she felt so grateful to finally be back in her old bedroom that she fell asleep and did not wake up for nearly 25 hours. No one accused the Stones of drugging their daughter this time, they were as baffled as Robert each time he came by to see if she was awake.

Robert met Miranda on the porch when she finally woke up enough to visit the next evening. He was surprised at the nerves he was feeling. He felt that they were close but they had a lot to work through. The fact that she was herself and not in Rachael anymore simplified things but it did not clarify everything.

When she stepped out of her parent's front door all his nerves dissolved and he just pulled her to him and held her close. It was so damn nice to have her in his arms again after so much confusion and fear. Neither even considered a kiss, the hug was more than enough at that moment.

"Miranda, I was so worried. I'm sorry this happened. I know he would have never got near you or Rachael if I did not leave you both," he was truly remorseful.

Miranda did not answer for a moment. She just sat on the swing and waited for Robert to join her. "In the hospital, I counted how often I thought about Conner before he snatched my body from the dorm. It had to have been in the thousands. Every day I found new ways to conjure him in my mind. Was he standing in the pickup line at Rachael's school? Did he find a way into my bedroom? If Kara or Rachael did not text or update social media for too long I knew they were captured. Once, a girl was out from school for a week with Mono, but I was convinced she was kidnapped. Every sound in the night and every stranger in the distance was Conner"

He held her hand and didn't interrupt.

"Do you know how many times I have thought about him since I came home?"

"I don't know."

"Twice. Once when my parents asked me about him, and once when I had to talk to the police. I slept soundly for the first time in what feels like forever and I feel like a weight has been lifted. I didn't even realize he was haunting me until he was gone. I don't feel the need to talk about him at all. Okay?"

Robert just nodded and sat and rocked in silence for a while. "Do you plan on returning to your dorm?" he finally asked.

"I do. I'm looking forward to it. Your genius sister kept my grades up and I think I want to start putting in time with the team to see if I have a shot for tryouts next year, even though this year is a bust for sure. What do you plan on doing?"

"I've been doing distance learning classes with Santa Fe and working my way up the East Coast, just kind of doing odd jobs and trying not to think of you and Rachael," Robert felt like he was confessing something, "Now I would like to get an apartment near you and see what happens."

"I would love that." Miranda scooted a little closer and Robert let out a breath he didn't even realize he was holding as he waited for her reply.

"I got into UF before all this went down, but I decided to stick to Santa Fe because I had to get away. Maybe if it all works out, and if they will still take me I'll join you there next term."

"I have not technically had my first day, you will have to ask Rachael if it is worth all the hype."

"I guess we will figure it out together then?"

"I like the sound of that." Miranda finally leaned up and kissed him, then they rocked on the porch and planned the near future until late into the night.

Chapter 55

I was not lying when I told Robert that I thought about Conner less now than I did before he took me to that cabin. In the months leading up to that night, I jumped at every shadow and he was in every fear I had. I brushed it aside, believing the detectives when they told my family that he would never return to this area. With the distraction of switching, seemingly permanently with Rachael, Robert leaving, and overall depression I guess I just became used to the fear of him.

Now as I settled into my first week of college while trying to look like this was all an old routine, I noticed the fear was gone. Now and then his melted face would flash before my eyes, but my deep secret was I did not feel remorse for what I did. I was equally horrified at the memory and horrified at my relief over the fact that Conner Adams could never get near me, Rachael, Kara, or any other girl again.

One day I noticed a familiar diamond tattoo on a girl in one of my classes, right next to her name on her wrist. When I asked her about it she just winked and said, "If you know, you know."

"I think I know. I saw this same tattoo on my own wrist once." I didn't know what else to say. If she slipped she would instantly know, if she didn't she would think I was weird but everyone was a little weird here. She winked at me and gathered her laptop and papers.

"Well, I guess you do know. We meet once a week." She pulled out a small black card with the same diamond symbol on one side and a QR code on the other. "I hope you come to our next meet-up, I could not imagine college without this group," she said earnestly after she handed it to me.

When I got back to my dorm room I scanned the code with my phone and opened a site with the words *Who are you today?* Written in red against a black background. In the bottom corner was a door. I clicked on it. This brought me to a new page that had three questions. With spots to type the answers.

1. What is your favorite thing about being who you are, today?
2. How long was the longest visit you have ever had?
3. What is something you dislike about who you are, today?

The questions were leading enough to weed out anyone who didn't have a clue about slipping. I answered them all a bit generically but also with enough information that they would know that I understood the meaning behind the words. After I hit submit the page went black. I clicked around but nothing happened so I set my phone on the desk and tried to study for midterms for classes I never attended. Rachael was coming next weekend to help me study as well but the odds were not in my favor when it came to acing them. I tried to focus on her notes and not on my phone screen. It took about thirty minutes before I heard a ding. When I picked up my phone it now said:

This Week's Meeting: Tuesday, 6:30 East Park - Bring Pie.

Bring pie? What kind of secret society asked for pie? I wrote the time down and put my phone in a drawer so I could actually study. By the time Tuesday rolled around I convinced Robert to come with me to this super-secret meeting. After all, who knows what these people wanted? It's not like slipping was a superpower but who knows how it could be exploited? I purchased an apple pie for me and a chocolate creme for Robert in case that was a form of admission.

Truly, I had no clue what to expect. We showed up at East Park right on time. I wondered if there would be more cloak and dagger hoops to jump through. A secret password, proof I could slip? Robert was on high alert as well. Until we came upon a group under one of the gazebos near the creek. There was a black banner with the diamond symbol in the center hanging up above a banquet of food. The bring pie was simply an invitation to add to the potluck. We added our pies to the dessert end, and the same girl who handed me the card came up and gave me a hug. She seemed much more open than she was in class.

"Who is this?" she held out her hand to Robert.

"I'm Robert. I'm here to make sure Miranda isn't pulled into some sort of scam." Robert eyed the group warily and a middle-aged man in a Gator's tank top and a pair of jorts laughed in his face.

"Naw, kid. We are just a family. Some of us don't get to be ourselves except when we are all together. At least it feels that way. If y'all want to come, then show up. We meet once a week and do these potlucks once a month."

A tall goth teenage boy piped in, "I made the website. We post the time and place there. Once we approve you the cookies in your computer will always get you in" he boasted then blushed bright red.

"I'm Melody," the girl from class introduced herself, and

then Robert and I did the same. The whole group welcomed us and told us to dig in, then went back to their busy chatter. It felt homey. Robert seemed less impressed, but to a girl who hid all her life, it was pretty epic.

"Sometimes we are more organized and actually discuss issues, but during the potlucks, it's more laid back," an elderly man sat down to eat next to me and Robert after we made our plates. "I'm Howard. I hope you both come back."

Robert just nodded. I had a feeling this was the start of something pretty cool.

"What do you discuss at the meetings?" I asked.

"Sometimes trading can get us in a pickle, like when my son Bryson flunked his final exam before Med school a few years back because he was not there to take it. Secret Societies across the globe are designed to help each other out. Without connections in here, he would never have been able to retake it without recourse. That's just my example. Trading can be difficult, it's nice to have a leg up where we can get it."

"I've always called it Sliding or Slipping," I confessed.

"Me too! I say I've just slipped out to my family when I get back. Trading seems so permanent I like sliding," Melody said from the next table over.

"Yeah, but think of how this sounds: Secret Society of Sliders. What are we incognito mini-sandwiches? Life Traders has a better ring," the goth kid who made the website pointed out. His name was Sam and he was the only one in his family to trade or slip as well.

I tried to imagine how nice it would have been to find this group in high school. It all sounded as ludicrous as it actually was to try to put a name on what we did but it was fun anyways. The pot-luck/super-secret society of sliders meeting was over before I knew it but I had a feeling I would be seeing a lot more of Melody at school. Robert agreed that he would return to each meeting with me by the time we left. We even discussed getting the name tattoos on our wrists but decided to maybe wait a little longer. He still liked keeping whoever slipped into him in the dark, and I had a terrible fear of needles. The concept seemed pretty cool though. I liked the idea of being able to identify others like me by the symbol. Aside from the needles, I didn't see a downside.

I never expected life to look so normal but by the time Robert drove away from my dorm that evening after getting kicked out by the RA at curfew and I texted my Mom that I loved her and goodnight I felt completely basic. I loved every second of it.

Epilogue

I can't tell the stories of all the people I slip into, but I'm finally developing the strength to tell my own. I'm Miranda Stone. I have been in countless lives and I still believe that everything we do matters. Even the little things each day create the habits that build our lives.

I was haunted by a man who plucked me up like a fruit ready to devour, now I am haunted by the knowledge that I can kill and feel no remorse. I was held down by loneliness and the burden of carrying my secrets, now I have a handsome boyfriend and a close circle of friends who know the real me. I once embraced the simple, now I understand that complexity may make life hard but it also makes it beautiful.

I would not trade a step of this journey or a moment of the past year. I am Miranda Stone, cheerleader, weirdo, and slider. I am finally starting to fill that bucket of mine with experiences that both terrify and thrill me one single drop at a time. Every experience I have may not be mine alone, but they are my own. I cannot tell the story of the lives I slip into but I can shape their story while creating my own.

Also by Amanda Harris

Once in a Blue June
Take a chance on a stranger and find out where it might lead
you on a hot summer night in this slow-burn sweet romance.

Hollow Harbor
Follow a mother and daughter as they go through a summer of
epic change in this cozy-mystery family drama.